"You need to learn how to mind your manners, Mahoney," Longarm said quietly.

"Maybe I can give you a few lessons on our way back to Denver," he continued.

"Well, I'll be damned if you don't sound like you're really one of the tough ones," the prisoner said. As he spoke he sat up and let the blanket drop away.

Although Longarm had seen several Wanted posters with artist's sketches of Chauncey Mahoney, alias the Stovespit Kid, he was not prepared for the Kid in the flesh.

Mahoney's face was fish-belly white. His brows were thick and beetling, his nose a shapeless blob that looked as pasty as his face. His lips were thick and blubbery, his chin grotesquely elongated, and when he twisted his face into a scowl as he gazed through the bars at Longarm, he showed a ragged set of snaggled teeth, two of the upper ones missing.

"All right," Mahoney sn_____ ____ look at me, if you've got to. Better m____ _____ be here later on. I've g_____ back to Denver."

--•TABOR EVANS•--

LONGARM

AND THE ESCAPE ARTIST

A JOVE BOOK

LONGARM AND THE ESCAPE ARTIST

A Jove Book/published by arrangement with
the author

PRINTING HISTORY
Jove edition/November 1986

ISBN: 0-515-08754-8

Chapter 1

When Longarm woke and saw how bright his room was there was no need for him to look out the window to discover the reason. Though according to his thinking it was far too early in the year for it to occur, that gleam was as familiar to his eyes as the threadbare nap of the faded carpet was to his feet when he rolled out of bed and started across the room. Too many times before he had seen that same brightness in the room, and knew what he would find.

In spite of that, he walked slowly to the window, picking up the bottle of Tom Moore Maryland rye from the dresser before pulling aside the tatter-edged window shade to glance outside. When he saw the brilliance of the clear early-day sky reflected from a thin coating of snow that covered the ground, he knew that he was seeing the official arrival of Denver's long winter.

It's a hell of a note, old son, he told himself after he had wiped his lips with the back of his hand following his eye-opener. *And there ain't much you nor nobody else can do about it. But if you was to hyper on to the office, maybe Billy Vail's got some kind of case that'll get you to Arizona or even down in the south part of Texas, where you'll have a chance to enjoy decent weather.*

Fishing out a long, slim cigar from the pocket of his vest, which hung in its accustomed place over the back of the chair beside his bed, he flicked his thumbnail over a match-head. He puffed until the cheroot was drawing satisfactorily, then began the familiar routine of checking his Colt and derringer before putting on his clothes. Finally dressed and ready, he

1

donned his long black coat before stepping out into the chilly air.

Snow's all right in its place, Longarm mused as he began taking long strides toward Cherry Creek. *But by rights it belongs at the North Pole, where there ain't no people for it to put out.*

Across the Colfax Street bridge the packed cinder pathway vanished and was replaced by the new red sandstone blocks which Denver's city fathers had just ordered installed. He started up the slanting intersection with Fourteenth Street. There had been enough pedestrian traffic to pack the snow-crust into a thin coating of slippery ice on the stones, and Longarm was forced to reduce his long strides to short, careful steps.

Chon Toy's restaurant was closed, but the place in the next block was open. After he had put down a platter of fried ham, eggs, and potatoes, washed down by two cups of strong black coffee, the day looked better in spite of the snow. Longarm covered the remaining distance to the federal building before he had finished his after-breakfast cheroot and mounted the marble steps of the stairway leading to the second floor.

With his stomach pleasantly full and the last inch of the cigar clamped between his strong teeth, he felt at peace with the world as he pushed through the office door. The young pink-cheeked clerk, Henry, glanced up as the door opened.

"Good morning, Marshal Long," he said. "Chief Marshal Vail's still downstairs in the telegraph room, but he said that I was to ask you to wait if you came in before he got back."

Longarm had already nodded an acknowledgement of the clerk's greeting. He said, "I reckon that means Billy's got a new case for me?"

"I'm not sure." The clerk frowned. "But the first thing he asked me to do this morning was to get him the file on Deputy Benson's murder, and he spent a lot of time going over it before he went down to the telegraph room."

"Was he acting like he'd got something new on that slippery son of a bitch that killed poor old Jed?"

"You know Marshall Vail as well as I do. When he doesn't

2

want to talk about something, wild horses couldn't drag a word out of him."

"I take that to mean he didn't say anything, then?"

"Not a word. And if you ask me—" Henry broke off as the door swung open and Vail came in.

"Glad to see you're almost on time for a change," he said to Longarm. "Come on in my office. I've got a new assignment for you that I want to talk about."

Following Vail across the room to the chief marshal's private office, Longarm remarked, "I hope this case you got in mind means you're sending me someplace where it's warm, Billy."

"That'd depend on what you call warm," Vail replied. His lips twitched with a suppressed smile. He had lost track of the number of times he'd heard Longarm's complaints about the Denver winters, and now repeated the offer that he'd made so often in the past. "Of course, if you're tired of the snow we get here in Denver, I can fix up a transfer for you to Tucson or El Paso or someplace where the winters are warmer."

"Well, I just might want to do that," Longarm replied, as he always did. "Let me think on it a spell."

"Sure." Vail nodded. "In the meantime, this little job I mentioned will get you out of the snow for a while."

Longarm drew his favorite red morocco upholstered chair up to the corner of Vail's paper-strewn desk and settled down. "Where're you sending me now?" he asked.

"Out to California. Oakland, to be exact."

"That means I got to buy me another can of flea powder," Longarm said. "I used up the last of what I had when I was on that O'Hara case in San Francisco."

"I'm sure you'll put it on your expense list," Vail told him. "You might even want to sprinkle some on the prisoner you're going to bring back. He jumps around like a flea, and from what I've heard he's just about as hard to catch up with."

"Wait a minute, Billy!" Longarm exclaimed. "If you're talking about who I think you are, I'm going out there to bring back the son of a bitch that gunned Jed Benson down!"

"That's right." Vail nodded. "The Stovespit Kid. And I

3

want him brought back here alive, so he can stand trial."

"Now, you know damn good and well I don't set up a prisoner the way some lawmen do," Longarm protested. "Let 'em think they're getting away and backshoot 'em when they start running."

"I'll give you that," Vail agreed. "But just the same, you close a lot of your cases with a pistol slug instead of an arrest warrant."

"I can't help it if a damned outlaw goes for his gun when I tell him to freeze," Longarm shot back. "But you can be real sure I'll bring that slippery bastard back on his own two feet. I want Ellie Benson to see him stand up in the dock when the judge tells him he's going to hang."

"Yes, I know you and Jed and Ellie were close friends," Vail said. "I counted Jed as my friend, too, and I feel just the same way you do about seeing the Stovespit Kid squirm when he gets sentenced. But don't forget for a minute how the Kid got the name he travels under."

Longarm nodded. "Sure. I never did happen to run across the slick son of a bitch before, but I know his reputation. From what I've heard, the Stovespit Kid's got a right to that name he travels under."

"Everybody that's ever had him in custody for more than ten minutes seems to agree that he's like a blob of spit on a hot stove," Vail smiled. "They say he can just about disappear even when you're looking right at him."

"I'd guess he's about the slickest getaway artist there ever was." Longarm frowned. "How many times has he got away from the law, Billy?"

"Twenty-three or twenty-four, according to his record," Vail replied. He picked up a sheaf of papers from the top of the heap that covered his desk and began thumbing through them. "I went over these yesterday evening when I got the telegram from the Oakland police chief saying they had the Kid in jail, but there's just too many for me to remember."

"I knew it was a bunch, but I didn't figure it was all that many," Longarm said. "But I'll be right careful to keep hold of him once I get my hands on him."

Vail nodded absently, his eyes still fixed on the papers in his hand.

Longarm asked, "Have you told Ellie yet?"

"Not yet," the chief marshal replied. He tossed the sheaf of documents on his desk and went on. "I thought that since you and Jed were such good friends, you might like to go with me when I tell her we've got the man who killed her husband."

Longarm recognized his chief's words for what they were, an unspoken plea for help in the most unpleasant task lawmen have to perform: discussing the death of one of their number with his widow. Though he had as little liking as Vail for such a visit, he nodded slowly.

"I reckon I better go with you, Billy. It's been a while since I've had time to visit Ellie. She's likely thinking both of us have forgot her, and it'll make her feel a lot better when she knows we've finally caught up with the murdering bastard that gunned Jed down."

Vail glanced at the Vienna Regulator clock that occupied a bracket shelf on the office wall. "It's a little too early for us to go out to Ellie's house right now," he said.

"Well, I got a mite of getting ready to do," Longarm suggested. "Suppose I go back to my room and put my travel gear in shape, and we can go out and visit Ellie later on."

"A good idea." Vail nodded. "Get back here in an hour or so. I'll have Henry write up your case orders and make up your travel vouchers while you're gone. Then, after we've had our visit with Ellie, I can drop you off at the depot on our way back to the office."

"I don't guess the government's ever going to boost our travel money any more than it's going to raise our pay, is it, Billy? Two cents a mile ain't such a much, especially since I got to buy grub out of it, too."

Vail shook his head. "Not a chance. If it makes you feel any better, though, I get the same travel allowance you do, and it puts me out of pocket the same way."

"Now, six cents a mile when I'm bringing back a prisoner ain't quite so bad," Longarm went on. "A man can make out on that, unless it's a short trip and you got more'n one pris-

5

oner to feed. But two cents . . ." He shook his head. "That just ain't enough, Billy, especially if it's a long railroad trip and you got to have a meal or two in the dining car."

"It just happens that this is something I agree with you about," Vail said. "I've argued over travel expenses with the men in Washington until I'm blue in the face, but I might as well be spitting into the wind for all the good it's done."

"Now that you mention spitting, how'd them fellows out in California ever get their hands on the Stovespit Kid?"

"That's something I can't answer," Vail admitted. "But if you haven't forgotten, when Ellie Benson described the man who gunned Jed down, it struck me that what she told us about him fitted the Kid, so I put his name on the fliers I sent out. Just guessing, I imagine the Oakland police caught him for a robbery or something in their area and matched him to the description on the fliers."

"I guess I'll have to wait till I get to California to find out," Longarm said, standing up. "I'll go get my gear, Billy. Look for me back in about two hours."

"Oh, I'm sure I can identify him all right," Ellie Benson said in response to Vail's question. "I'll never forget that man's ugly face as long as I live!"

"Seeing her husband get gunned down ain't something a smart lady like Ellie would be apt to forget, Billy," Longarm told Vail.

"Just the same, it's been nearly six months since Jed was killed," the chief marshal replied. "And I want Ellie to read the description of the Stovespit Kid on this flier." As he was speaking, Vail took the Wanted notice from his pocket and unfolded it, then handed it to her. "Now, you go over it, Ellie, and be absolutely positive that the man described on it is the one you saw. I need to be sure about everything connected with this case before Long gets on that train to California."

Ellie smoothed out the flier and read it while Longarm and Vail watched her, both of them trying to gauge her reactions as she read not only the description of the Stovespit Kid, but a condensed version of the events before and after her husband's murder.

Ellie Benson was in her middle or late thirties. Her facial features were something between what some would call pretty and what others might describe as handsome. She still wore widow's weeds, the black satin of her dress matching the smooth sheen of her hair, which she wore pulled back without a center part and coiled in a bun at the nape of her neck. Her dark eyes, dry in spite of her obvious agitation at being reminded of her husband's death, moved along the lines of the text on the flier. When she had finished reading it, she nodded positively.

"This certainly fits the man I saw kill Jed," she told them. "Even though I was all upset at the time, I'll never forget his ugly face."

"Maybe you better go over what happened again, too," Longarm suggested. "It's been a while since—" He stopped and made a fresh start. "I'd imagine you was pretty much upset at the time, and you might remember something now that you missed when you was telling Billy about it before."

"There really isn't all that much to remember," Ellie said slowly. "You'd put Jed on bailiff duty that week, Billy, and I'd looked for him to come home right after court adjourned. But he didn't get home when I expected him, and after I'd waited for a while I thought maybe he'd stopped in at the saloon down at the corner of Twenty-first and Lawrence." She turned to Longarm and went on, "You know how he'd do, sometimes."

"Sure," Longarm nodded. "When Jed used to ask me to come eat supper with you and him, he always wanted to stop for a drink there. I reckon he'd go in just the same when he was coming home by himself."

"He did," Ellie agreed, "but he never stayed very long at the saloon, just enough time for one or two drinks."

"Go on," Vail said quietly after Ellie had stopped talking and sat silently for several moments. "I know it's not easy for you to go over this again, Ellie, but it's important."

"Yes, I understand that, Billy," she replied. "I'm doing the best I can." She straightened up in her chair and went on. "I was still a little way from the saloon when I saw a man come out. I didn't pay that much attention to him, because he turned

7

down the street the same way I was going, so all I saw was his back. Then, before I got to the saloon, Jed came out and I stopped, because I thought he would turn the way I was coming from and I'd just wait for him. But he started after the man who'd come out of the saloon a minute earlier." She paused again.

"That's the one you identified as the Stovespit Kid," Longarm prompted her.

"Yes. That was later on, of course. When I saw Jed turn the wrong way, I couldn't understand it. I was too far away to call him without... well, without making a big disturbance right there in the street. At least, that was what was in my mind right then. So I started following him."

"While Jed was following the Stovespit Kid," Vail said.

She nodded. "But I didn't know then that Jed was following him, or anybody else. I wasn't thinking about much of anything except that something was going on that I didn't understand."

"That's easy to figure out," Longarm nodded. "Jed turning the wrong way and all."

"I was really wondering," Ellie said. "And I guess I was getting a mite upset. Jed was moving pretty fast. I had to hurry to catch up with him, but before I could get close enough to call him without bellowing, the man Jed was after turned around and saw him. And then everything happened so fast that I got all confused."

Ellie broke off her narrative when Longarm and Vail exchanged frowning glances.

"Was that when you saw the Stovespit Kid shoot Jed?" Longarm asked.

"Yes, it was. I think he'd caught on by then that Jed was after him. Anyhow, he turned around, and I didn't see the gun he had in his hand until he shot Jed. When Jed fell down, the fellow you call the Stovespit Kid started running. I did, too, of course, but I was running to see how bad Jed was hurt, and that Kid fellow was running away."

"You didn't chase him, of course?" Vail asked.

"What good could I have done, Billy? I didn't have a gun.

8

I guess I could've taken Jed's pistol, but I just plain didn't think about it. All I was interested in was my husband lying there on the ground."

"Sure. I understand that, Ellie." Vail nodded.

"And Jed was dead when you got to him, you said?" Longarm asked her.

"Not right that minute. He said something to me that I didn't understand, but afterward, when I thought it all out, I realized what he said was the name of the man he was after. And when Jed got the name out he sort of moaned and died."

"By this time the Stovespit Kid was long gone, I guess?" Vail asked.

"I guess so. I wasn't thinking about him, Billy. I was too worried about Jed to think of anything else. It wasn't until later on, when you'd described the man to me, that I realized who he was."

"But you're still sure he was the one you saw?" Longarm asked.

"Of course I am!" Ellie replied indignantly. "It was still daylight when you and Billy got there from the office, after the city policemen went after you. And that was maybe half an hour after Jed got shot."

"So it was." Longarm nodded. "You'd oughta remember that, too, Billy. We come out here together, after the city policeman had brought Ellie home. There was still light enough to see by even after we got here."

"Oh, I remember what I saw," Vail replied. "But I'm not the one who's going to have to testify in court after you bring the Stovespit Kid back here and he goes on trial. It's Ellie's memory we'll be depending on for a conviction."

"Well, you don't have to worry about me, Billy," Ellie said positively. "I don't guess I'll ever forget that day."

"I don't guess you will, at that," Vail agreed. "But we don't want to risk seeing the Stovespit Kid get off because some jury doesn't believe what you remember."

"You believe me, don't you?" she asked.

"Why, sure. But I'm what judges call a prejudiced witness. It's my business to bring criminals into court. Your testimony is what's going to send the Stovespit Kid to the gallows."

"And that's just where he ought to go!" Ellie exclaimed.

"Now, Billy ain't arguing that," Longarm said quickly. "I know what he's driving at, and he's right." He turned to Vail. "I guess you're satisfied that Ellie's story's going to hold up, Billy? Because if you are, I sure don't want to miss my train."

"I'm satisfied." Vail nodded, standing up. "Ellie, I did hate to bother you with all this, and bring back sad memories, but I guess you understand why I had to."

"Of course I do, Billy," she said. "And it wasn't all that bad after I got started. Don't you worry. I won't forget any of what I saw when I get into court."

A light snow had begun falling when Longarm and Vail got outside. Longarm stopped on the porch long enough to pull up the collar of his coat before stepping down to the street.

As he and Vail started for the depot, Longarm said, "You know, Billy, I'm real glad you picked me out for this job. The way it looks now, the weather here's going to get worse before it gets better, and it don't snow around San Francisco Bay. I'll bet the most snow I'm going to see before I get back will be when the train goes across Donner Pass."

Chapter 2

By the time Longarm stepped off the train in the Burlington Depot in Cheyenne, the early snow flurries had been left behind and the night sky was clear. Each star in the rich blue curtain overhead glowed sharply defined in the crisp air. As he walked with long, easy strides along the station platform, he glanced into the lighted windows of the depot's restaurant. The supper rush had ended and most of the tables were unoccupied. He got a glimpse of a waiter putting a platter of richly browned steak on one of the tables, and suddenly his stomach reminded him that it had been a long time since lunch.

With almost two hours to wait for the Union Pacific Limited that would take him on the next stage of his long trip, Longarm decided to eat supper before claiming his baggage and lugging it across town. Smoothing his steerhorn moustache with a fingertip, he pushed through the door into the café and sat down at the nearest vacant table. A waiter rushed up with a menu and pulled out a chair, and Longarm settled into it.

A glance at the price of steak changed Longarm's mind about his half-formed dinner plans. He was studying the price column, trying to reconcile his appetite with his two-cents-per-mile travel allowance, when the waiter returned.

"Looks like I'm going to have to settle for—" Longarm began, but the waiter interrupted him.

"Excuse me, sir, but I didn't come to take your order," the man said. "The lady at that corner table asked me to invite you to join her."

Glancing in the direction indicated by the waiter's nod, Longarm frowned. The corner table was occupied by a woman whose face was vaguely familiar. Longarm was sure he'd seen

11

her before, but he couldn't recall the place or the occasion. When she saw him looking at her, the woman nodded and smiled. Her face still hung in Longarm's memory, as did her smile and the manner in which she moved her head, but no name popped into his mind. Never one to hesitate over a decision, he stood up and started toward her table.

"Marshal Long!" the mystery woman exclaimed as Longarm reached the table and stopped beside it. "I'm so glad you accepted my invitation. Please sit down." When Longarm hesitated, she went on, "It's been such a long time that I was afraid you'd forgotten me, but I'll never forget how you saved me from that awful outlaw up in the Divide."

Memory rushed back into Longarm's mind, the recollection of a case when he'd trailed a kidnapper into the Medicine Bow Mountains and rescued his victim, the daughter of Arthur Mason, Wyoming Territory's federal land commissioner. He recognized the young woman now, though she had changed a bit from the half-naive girl who'd shared his bedroll after inviting him to join her in bathing in an icy mountain pool.

"Why, I was just doing my job," he said. "But it sure is nice to see you again, Miss Mason."

"Please sit down," she repeated, and as Longarm hung his hat on the wall hook and pulled out a chair, she went on, "But it's not Betty Mason now. It's Betty Colyer."

"Stands to reason," Longarm commented as he settled into the chair. "As pretty a girl as you was bound to get married."

A shadow crossed Betty Colyer's face, and was banished almost instantly by a smile. "Married and widowed," she said. "But all that's past me now. I suppose you're on your way to save some other poor damsel in distress?"

"I'm starting out on another case," Longarm replied, "but it ain't like the one you got in mind."

"Then perhaps you'll join me for supper and tell me about your new case while we eat. You see, I was supposed to meet my father here at the depot and have dinner with him, but when I got here there was a telegram waiting for me saying he'd been held up in Laramie and won't be back until tomorrow."

12

"I guess he's a pretty busy man," Longarm remarked, "just like he always has been."

"Oh, he'd be unhappy if he wasn't busy. But since he had already arranged for our dinner and paid for it when he made the arrangements I decided the best thing to do was to stay and eat. Then I saw you, and I thought it would be nice to have company. You will have dinner with me, I hope?"

Longarm suppressed the sigh of relief that he felt rising. Since sitting down, he'd been remembering the prices on the menu and juggling his two-cents-a-mile travel allowance against the cost of a dinner for two. A dinner paid for by the Territory's well-financed land commissioner was another matter. He said, "Well, now, since you've been nice enough to invite me, I'd be a pretty sorry specimen if I turned you down. There ain't a thing I'd like better, Miz Colyer."

"Now, let's don't have any more 'Mrs. Colyer,' Longarm," she said with a mocking sternness in her voice. "You see, I remember your nickname, as well as a lot of other things about that time when you rescued me."

Before Longarm could reply, the waiter returned carrying soup bowls, and during the remainder of the meal he and Betty Colyer chatted about everything except their first meeting in the high, craggy spine of the Medicine Bows. From the looks Betty aimed at him from time to time, Longarm sensed that he was not alone in remembering that encounter. Betty's occasional smiling silences told him that she was also thinking of the night that followed their first encounter and of the two nights they had shared on their long ride back to Cheyenne.

In spite of his charming companion, Longarm had not lost track of the time. He was well aware that the westbound Union Pacific train he had planned to catch had passed through Cheyenne about the time he and Betty were finishing their steaks. Without glancing at his watch, he reminded himself that there would be another UP Limited in the middle of the morning, and on such a long trip a delay of a few hours wasn't all that important, with the Stovespit Kid safe in a cell in the Oakland jail.

"You were planning to stop here overnight, weren't you?"

13

Betty asked in a casual voice as she put down her drained coffee cup. "At least, that was the impression I got."

"Well, I'll tell you, Betty, I hadn't figured on running into you here, so I was aiming to catch the westbound night express on the Union Pacific."

"But that train went through Cheyenne almost an hour ago, and there won't be another westbound express until late tomorrow morning!"

"Sure. I know that, but like I told you during supper, all I'm going to do in California is get that prisoner and bring him back. That ain't like trying to find a trail to follow when I'm after some killer or big-time crook on the loose, and I figured I'd rather visit with you than be in such an all-fired hurry to move on."

"I see you haven't lost your ability to guess what I'm thinking," Betty smiled. "And since we've finished dinner, why don't we go home now?"

"There ain't a thing I'd like better," Longarm told her. As they started for the door, he added, "I imagine we can find a hack waiting outside the depot."

"My buggy's at the hitch rail, so we don't have to worry about a hack. But if you don't mind, I'll have to ask you to unhitch the horse when we get to my house."

"As long as I don't have to groom the critter, that won't bother me one bit," Longarm said as he handed Betty into the buggy. "And it won't take me but a minute to do a simple little chore like that."

Betty Colyer's house was a two-story structure standing on an avenue of wide-spaced dwellings, and like its neighbors it spoke of a solid financial status rather than great wealth. Night lights glowed softly through two or three of the windows, one shining from a rear window serving to light their way as they walked arm-in-arm from the stable to the house.

"I hope you won't mind going in through the back door," Betty said as they mounted the steps.

"Not a bit."

"I don't hire any full-time household help," Betty went on, opening the door and motioning for Longarm to go in. "Just a cleaning woman who comes in twice a week and a man who

14

cleans up the stable and yard every week. We'll be just as much alone as we were when you were bringing me home from the Medicine Bows, but this time we'll be a lot more comfortable."

"Well, I don't recall that being a mite cold and not having anything but a blanket between us and the ground kept us from enjoying ourselves," he said.

"No." She smiled, turning back to face Longarm after locking the door. "And I've never forgotten those nights, Longarm."

As she spoke, Betty stepped up to Longarm. He took her in his arms and she turned her lips up to meet his. They clung in a fervid embrace while their questing tongues entwined, Betty pressing her hips close to him, rubbing against his growing erection. She dropped her hand to feel Longarm's stiffening shaft and a soft moan began bubbling in her throat. When they broke their kiss, breathless after their prolonged embrace, she smiled at him and stepped away to blow out the lamp.

"I'm not a little girl any more," she said. "I've learned a great deal since our nights in the mountains. I can't wait for us to get upstairs to my bedroom."

"You lead the way, Betty," Longarm told her. "I'm right with you."

When Longarm followed Betty into the bedroom, he saw the glow of embers from a dying fire in a fireplace that was centered in the wall opposite the big double bed. A lamp was burning on the dresser, and he leaned forward to blow it out, but she said, "Don't. I want to see you, even if that lamp's not quite as romantic as the moonlight we had before."

"It'll do just as good," Longarm told her. He took off his gunbelt and hung it over the back of the chair that stood within arm's reach of the bed, the butt of the Colt within easy grasp.

Betty had begun undressing the moment they entered the room. Her fingers moved quickly, and she let her dress fall to the floor where she was standing, just inside the door.

Longarm wasted no time in starting to shed his clothes after his gunbelt was out of the way. He levered out of his boots, then, like Betty, let the rest of his garments fall to the floor. He speeded up when he saw Betty's fingers releasing the hooks and eyes that closed the front of her camisole, her arms pulling the garment's soft fabric tightly against it and emphasizing the swell of her full breasts.

Betty looked up and noticed that Longarm had stripped to his balbriggans. She stopped her own undressing to watch him, her eyes fixed on the bulging erection that swelled out at his crotch. Bending forward, he slid his undersuit over his hips and leaned forward to pull his feet free from its clinging cuffs.

"My memory wasn't playing tricks on me," she gasped. "You really *are* as big as I remembered!"

"Growing up ain't changed you as far as I can see," Longarm told her. "You're even prettier than when you was just a girl turning into a woman."

"I've learned more than I knew then," Betty said. "It takes a girl a while to turn into a woman." She moved to stand in front of Longarm. "And I've learned a lot more about the things men enjoy." She smiled. "Shall we go to bed?" she asked.

"I always let the lady call the tune she wants to dance to," Longarm told her.

"Then let's dance in bed for a while," she said, rising to her feet.

He plunged into her with one long thrust and began stroking vigorously while soft cries of pleasure flowed from her lips. She locked her ankles over Longarm's back and brought her hips up to meet his lusty thrusts.

Her body was beginning to quiver. Longarm began speeding up the tempo of his thrusting as Betty's quivers became body-wrenching shudders and little cries of pleasure poured from her throat. He raced to meet her climax, and as Betty screamed ecstatically Longarm let himself go with a final series of thrusts. He slowed his thrusting then to slow, relaxed strokes as he carried Betty through her writhing, jerking spasm, and as it faded he let himself relax and lie quietly on her soft body.

For a while they did not speak. Then Betty stirred and Longarm lifted his torso and stretched his arms to hold himself poised above her without breaking the bond of flesh that still connected them.

"Was I getting too heavy for you?" he asked.

Betty looked up at him, her blue eyes gleaming, her full red lips curled in the beginning of a smile. She shook her head and said, "Not a bit. I love to feel your weight on me again, Longarm." Her smile grew mischievous. "Do you still remember how it was that first time?"

"Like it was yesterday. There I was, standing knee-deep in that ice-cold pond up in the Medicine Bows, and holding you up, all wet and shivering."

"You weren't exactly dry yourself," she reminded him. "But you certainly did warm me up."

"Well, if you remember it the way I do, you done a pretty good job of warming me up at the same time."

They decided to celebrate their reunion with a drink. Longarm fished one of his long, thin cigars out of his vest pocket and trailed a thin stream of smoke down the stairs when he went for the liquor. Returning to the bedroom, carrying a bottle of rye whiskey and glasses, he found Betty standing in front of the dresser, looking at her reflection in its wide mirror.

"Do you like me as much as you did when I was a green and silly little girl?" she asked.

"Better," he replied. "The way I recall that time, you never was silly, Betty. And you was pretty then, but now you're a whole lot prettier."

Putting the bottle and glasses on the dresser, Longarm cupped Betty's full breasts in his hands and bgan rubbing his iron-hard thumb over their pink rosettes. Betty turned her head to offer him her lips, and trailed one hand down to grasp his flaccid shaft. As they held their kiss, she tightened her hand on him, and began gently squeezing and releasing the quiescent flesh in a rhythmic motion. She sighed in her throat when she felt him swelling in response to her subtle caresses.

"Let the drinks wait," she whispered.

Longarm agreed. "We've got all the time in the world, Betty. My train don't leave until noon tomorrow."

* * *

Longarm was waiting at the Union Pacific depot the following day when the westbound Limited came to a halt with a metallic sigh of its brakes followed by the loud hiss of escaping steam as the engineer flushed the locomotive's cylinders. Picking up his saddlebags and rifle, Longarm started walking along the depot platform toward the passenger coaches. He reached the second coach, where the conductor stood helping the departing passengers to step to the platform, and joined the three or four men who were waiting to get on the train.

"All the way to the end of the line, I see," the conductor remarked when Longarm showed his ticket. "You'll have to let the brakeman pick up that rifle and put it in the baggage car after the train starts."

"Now, I never had to do that before," Longarm protested.

"It's a new company rule," the trainman replied. "There's been too much shooting out of the coach windows lately. It was all right back in the days when the only animals we saw along the right-of-way were buffalo, but now there's so many ranches sprung up that the owners have been complaining about passengers shooting their cattle."

"Eastern tenderfeet." Longarm nodded. "Can't say I blame the ranchers." As he spoke, Longarm was taking out his wallet. He flipped it open to show his badge. "I'm a deputy United States marshal, travelling on a case. Does that make any difference?"

"Well, now." The conductor frowned. "That new rule doesn't say anything about exceptions, but the stationmaster's standing right over there. If you don't mind, Marshal, you might step over and have a word with him. I'll join you as soon as I'm sure all the other passengers have boarded."

Longarm found the stationmaster polite but adamant in refusing to break the new rule without authorization from the UP's head office. "I'm sure they didn't intend to include rifles a lawman might be carrying," he said. "But until I can wire them and they come back with an answer, I'm just going to have to ask you to let the baggagemaster look after that rifle, Marshal."

18

Reluctantly, Longarm surrendered his Winchester and got on the train. He was the last passenger aboard, and as he walked back through the coaches looking for a seat on the crowded train, he stopped in astonishment when he saw a familiar face in the third coach.

Ellie Benson was sitting halfway down the car, staring out the window at the busy Union Pacific yards as she waited for the train to start.

Chapter 3

Absorbed in watching the activities of the yard crews and the switch engine spotting and shifting boxcars, Ellie did not see Longarm until he had walked down the aisle and stopped beside her seat. Then she turned and looked at him and her jaw dropped.

"Longarm!" she exclaimed. "You were supposed to be on the train that left yesterday!"

"I was for a fact," he agreed. Sliding into the vacant seat beside Ellie, he leaned back against its green plush upholstery and shoved his booted feet under the seat ahead. When he was comfortably settled, he went on, "And you're supposed to be in Denver."

"Yes," she agreed, refusing to meet Longarm's eyes. After a long pause, when he did not question her further, she went on, "I got tired of looking at four walls in an empty house, Longarm. I thought a little trip might help me get used to being a widow."

"It ain't any of my business, Ellie," Longarm said, trying to choose his words carefully, "but I don't guess you'd mind telling me where you're taking your little trip to."

Again Ellie was slow in answering. "I—I really don't have anyplace special in mind. Just a trip. Someplace for a change of scenery."

"Well, now, you had to buy a ticket to that someplace, it don't make much difference where it is. Suppose you tell me just what it says on your train ticket."

Ellie's silence was unusually long this time. Longarm sat patiently, waiting, while she frowned and fidgeted in her seat.

"Oakland," she said at last, her voice barely above a whisper.

"How'd you happen to pick Oakland out of all the places you could get to on this train?"

"Why . . ." Ellie frowned for a moment, and Longarm was sure she was searching her mind for a reason to give him. At last she said triumphantly, "I bought my ticket to the end of the line, that's all. Don't you see, I can get off anyplace where I feel like I want to stop."

Longarm shook his head. "Now, you think back a little bit, Ellie," he said, keeping his voice soft and level. "You've heard me and Jed talking a lot of times about cases we been on. You're bound to remember hearing one of us say we knew when somebody wasn't telling us the truth."

Ellie made no reply. She stared at the back of the seat ahead, refusing to meet Longarm's eyes.

"You might as well make up your mind to answer my question," Longarm said quietly after several moments had passed. "Or maybe it'd be easier if I just told you what I was thinking." When Ellie still didn't respond, he went on, "You're heading for Oakland because that's where the Stovespit Kid's in jail. And I bet if I was to look in your valise, I'd find you got one of Jed's pistols put away in it. You're aiming to shoot the Stovespit Kid before I can get him back to Denver to stand trial. Ain't that the fact of the matter, Ellie?"

After she had maintained her silence for another minute or two, Ellie nodded slowly. Turning to face Longarm, she said, "I guess I ought to've known better than to try to fool you. But I didn't expect to run into you, Longarm! You're supposed to be on the train that left Denver yesterday!"

"Something happened that made me chance my plans," Longarm told her. "But that wouldn't've made no real difference."

"What do you mean?" she frowned.

"You couldn't've got away with killing the Stovespit Kid, Ellie. All you might've done was get yourself into a heap of trouble that you can do without."

"Oh, I'd've figured out a way," Ellie replied, her voice still hard and stubborn. "I'd have killed that murdering little crook just like he killed my husband!"

"And if you'd done that, I'd've had to let the Oakland

police arrest you and maybe I'd have to testify against you when your case went to court," Longarm pointed out. "You know that, Ellie. It don't matter that Jed was just about the best friend I had. I'd've still had to do my sworn duty."

"I guess I didn't think about that," she said soberly. "All I could think about was getting even."

"Getting even is what the law does for you," Longarm reminded her. "Now, let's talk about what you're going to do next."

"I suppose I'll have to go back home," Ellie said, after a moment's thought. "I know I can't go on with what I'd planned to do, now that you've figured it out."

"That sounds sensible," Longarm agreed. "And you might as well make up your mind to—

Ellie broke in. She said, "Oh, I've already make up my mind. I'm not going to play the fool, Longarm, and I don't want to make any trouble for you."

"You'll go on back to Denver, then?" When Ellie nodded, he went on, "I'll talk to the conductor and fix it up so you can change your ticket."

"Since I'm gong back, I'd like to get off as soon as I can," she said. "Go ahead and see what you can arrange."

"That's real smart, Ellie," Longarm told her. "We'll be pulling into Rock Springs pretty soon, now. I'll go find the conductor and see what he can fix up for you."

His legs cramped after sitting in the railroad coach during the long, uneventful hours after Ellie had gotten off the train, Longarm looked out the coach window as he heard the engine's whistle sound the quick triple tattoo that announced a station stop was just ahead. For most of the morning the train had been crawling down switchbacks and sharp curves on the winding track through the Wasatch Range, but for the past three-quarters of an hour it had been rolling across the wide alluvial plain that surrounded the Great Salt Lake.

Brakes rasped with the muted shriek of metal grinding against metal. Longarm stood up as the Limited slowed down, then creaked and squealed to a halt in front of the Brigham City depot. The conductor, a harried look on his face, came hurrying up the aisle just as Longarm started to step out himself, and their legs somehow got entangled for a moment.

"Sorry, Marshal Long," the trainman said. "I was thinking about a problem we're having, and didn't watch where I was going."

"Nothing serious, I hope," Longarm said.

"Oh, nothing that can't be cured. If you've made this trip before, you'll know that we got onto Western Pacific trackage out of Ogden, and we'll roll on their rail the rest of the way. But for some reason, the stationmaster just handed me a flimsy from the section superintendent ordering me to stop here and hold the train until I get a wire from him clearing me to go on."

Longarm broke in to say, "I understand a little bit about railroads, after all the train riding I have done. That's going to throw your whole schedule outa kilter, ain't it?"

"That's right. And I don't know the reason, so I'm going to have to wire the super and find out why."

"Looks like we'll just be setting here a while, then?"

"We might wait ten minutes, but it might be an hour or more," the trainman replied. "I won't know until the general superintendent sends me a message to highball."

"You think we'll be here long enough for me to walk over to the closest saloon and have a drink, and see if I can buy a bottle of rye whiskey?"

"I guess you've forgotten where we are," the conductor said with a smile. "You're in Mormon country now, Marshal. They don't let any whiskey sellers set up shop here in Utah Territory."

"That had slipped my mind, all right," Longarm said. "And I drained the bottle I brought along someplace in that stretch we just crossed over."

"I'm afraid you'll have to wait until we're past the Great Salt Lake," the conductor went on. "You might not have noticed it, but we cut the dining car off at Rock Springs. The brass won't risk some passenger bribing a waiter to slip him a drink while we're going through this section."

"Well, if you think I got time for a little stroll, I'd sure like to get the kinks outa my legs."

"I'll be at the telegraph desk in the depot for ten or fifteen minutes, at least," the conductor said. "Just keep your eyes on the station, and start back when I come out. We'll have to make up the time we're losing, and we'll be highballing out of here as soon as I get the word."

"I'll keep an eye peeled," Longarm said, "and soon as I see you come outa the depot, I'll head for the train."

Swinging off the coach vestibule, Longarm crossed the track between the motionless train and the depot and angled toward the street just ahead. He stopped at the edge of the board sidewalk and looked up and down the deserted street. The depot stood just inside the town's boundaries, and to his right he could see some scattered residences.

Trying to decide which direction he wanted to take, he looked down the street in the opposite direction. A short distance from where he stood, Longarm saw signs extending over the sidewalk above the doors of stores and business buildings. He turned toward the commercial district and started walking, but he had taken only a few steps before he stopped, frowning.

There was something strange about the thoroughfare. Though the hour was almost noon, a time when there should be buggies and wagons and people bustling about, not a person nor a vehicle was in sight.

Old son, Longarm told himself, *something ain't right about this place. Brigham City ain't such a much for size, but it just don't stand to reason that everybody in town decided to stay home today. If it was a Sunday, them streets looking the way they do now might make sense, but here it is, Saturday at high noon. That's a time of day when this street oughta be buzzing like a beehive.*

Longarm was still standing at the edge of the sidewalk trying to puzzle it out when he heard the conductor's voice hailing him.

"Marshal Long!" the trainman called. "Would you step over here for a minute?"

When Longarm turned, he saw that the conductor was not alone. A second man, wearing a leather vest and tight-fitting

24

trousers, stood beside the trainman. As he started walking toward the pair, Longarm saw a silver star gleaming on the man's vest. He moved a bit faster.

"This is Jim Holden, Marshal," the conductor said. "He's the town marshal here in Brigham City. I mentioned you to him when we met in the depot, and he'd like a word with you."

"Glad to make your acquaintance, Holden," Longarm said, extending his hand.

"That goes for me, too," Holden said as they shook. "Of course, I've heard a lot about you, if you're the one they call Longarm."

"I answer to the name," Longarm nodded. Then, with a gesture that took in the street and the center of Brigham City, he went on. "I was just standing there wondering what's going on in this town of yours."

"Outlaws," Holden said succinctly. "A couple of train robbers that got into a shooting scrape up in a little place north of here, called Corrine."

"And you figure they're heading this way?"

"They was when they left Corrine. The marshal from up there took after 'em, but he lost 'em someplace along the way."

"How'd he come to do that?"

"Damned if I know, Marshal Long. Pete Calder, he's the town marshal up there, figures they might've left the road on some trail that'd take 'em to a hideout. That country up there around Corrine shelters a lot of outlaws. Always has. But he figures they won't stay anyplace, they'll be cutting a shuck for the railroad line to get as far away as they can."

"Well, that makes sense," Longarm said. "And that's why you closed your town down?"

Holden nodded. "I figured we'd have a better chance to get 'em if there wasn't a lot of people milling around."

"They're bad outlaws, then?"

"Bad enough. They held up a Colorado & Southern train down south of Denver and got clear away with a big heap of loot. Pete says they rode off from the job with more than a

25

hundred thousand dollars, mostly gold in sacks outa the express car, and maybe another fifty thousand in money and jewelry from the passengers."

"That's why we got sidetracked here," the conductor broke in. "Soon as Calder found out who those three fellows were, he wired the WP main office to put all us trainmen on the lookout. The division super figured we'd better not take on that stretch north of the Great Salt Lake while they were on the loose."

"Hold on," Longarm frowned. "You're talking about three outlaws now, but a minute ago Holden said two. Not that it makes such a never mind, but which is it?"

"There's two still loose," Holden replied. "One of 'em was cut down when they tried to rob the bank up at Corrine. Calder's got him in jail up there. The other ones got clear away."

"If they'd made such a real haul when they held up that train, why'd they bother with a little back-country bank?" Longarm frowned. "Seems to me they'd've just laid low for a spell."

"These fellows ain't very smart, Longarm," Holden grinned. "It seems they buried their loot on the way up to Corrine, just kept out enough for travelling money. Then they went busted in a poker game and to save going back to where they'd cached their money they tried to rob the bank."

Longarm nodded. "Sounds sorta familiar. I've seen enough outlaws to believe every word of it."

"Well, that's about the size of it," Holden went on. "One of 'em got shot up pretty bad, and he's in jail now up at Corrine. Pete got the names of the other two from the one he's got in jail up there, and he found out they was planning to double back to the railroad and get clear out of this part of the country, so he took out after them."

"You know who they are, then."

"Oh, sure," Holden nodded. "Their names are Gene Wright and Oscar Weatherell. The third one's going under the name of George Tipton. He's the one that got shot up, and he's in the lockup in Corrine now."

"So that's how you happen to know so much about it,"

Longarm nodded thoughtfully. "That Tipton must've done considerable talking."

"He did," Holden replied. "And that's one reason I'm so damned set on finding his friends. The three of 'em buried the loot from that holdup in Colorado someplace close to Corrine, up along the Bear River."

"I guess the Colorado & Southern's got a pretty good-sized reward out for them?" Longarm suggested.

"If you're interested, the railroad's offering five thousand apiece for 'em," Holden said. "That's one reason I asked the conductor to call you over. If we get the two crooks that's supposed to be heading down here, and there's one in jail in Corrine, that'd be an easy five thousand apiece for us two and Calder."

"You must be new at being a lawman, Holden," Longarm said. "Or you'd know federal deputies can't take reward money. Not that it'd make any never mind, if you're figuring on asking me to give you and your friend Calder a hand."

"If they pick up some more of their kind, the way Pete says they might, your help will sure come in handy," Holden told him.

"Hold on, Marshal Long," the conductor broke in. "I was on a clear wire to the general super's office when Marshal Holden came in to tell me what he just told you. Since there's not much chance the outlaws are ahead of us, the super cancelled his layover order. He figures there's not any danger up ahead, so we'll be pulling out as quick as we can after I get the word back to the engine crew."

"Well, I guess that ends any chance that you'll be able to help us over the hump with those outlaws," Holden said to Longarm. "I wouldn't expect you to let your own case go while you stopped and gave us a hand."

"Don't get too previous, Holden," Longarm told him. He turned to the conductor and asked, "There'll be another west-bound Limited along tomorrow, I guess?"

"Of course. The Limiteds run on a daily schedule."

"Then, if I stay here and give Holden and his friend a hand, I suppose I can get on tomorrow's train," Longarm said thoughtfully.

27

"Sure you can, Marshal," the conductor nodded. "All I have to do is punch up a layover ticket for you."

"What about the case you're on, Marshal Long?" Holden asked. "I don't want to be messing you up on it."

"You won't be," Longarm replied. "It ain't like I got to be in all that much of a hurry to get to California. All I'm going out there for is to pick up a prisoner who's in the Oakland jail and take him back to Denver to stand trial."

"You'll stay, then?" Holden asked.

"If you need me to help you, I'd say I got a duty to stay," Longarm nodded. He turned to the conductor. "Me and the town marshal will have to talk a minute, so I'll take it right kindly if you'll get your baggageman to bring me my rifle, and see that my gear gets stowed away in the station."

"Of course," the trainman agreed quickly. As he turned to hurry away, he added over his shoulder, "And I'll leave your layover ticket with the stationmaster."

Nodding to the conductor, Longarm said to Holden, "Now, then. I guess you and your friend have got a plan worked up to trap the train robbers?"

"Sort of," the lawman replied. "We figure they'll be wanting to move fast, which means they won't waste time trying to circle off the road through that rough country. They know they give us the slip, and they'll likely make it back to the road and head this way as soon as they can."

"So Calder's gone up the road, he'll lay low till they get past him, and you'll stay here." Longarm frowned. "That way you'll have 'em pinned down between you and get 'em in a crossfire."

"Sounds like you've figured the same way we did," Holden said. "Have you got a better idea?"

Longarm shook his head. "Your scheme sounds all right to me. I don't guess your friend Calder's trigger-happy, is he?"

"If you're worrying about him mistaking you for one of the outlaws, they'll be mounted and Pete knows I'll be afoot," the Brigham City marshal pointed out. "He won't take a shot at you by mistake."

"That's what I had in mind," Longarm said. "Let's get started, then. I'll go on up the road from town a ways past

28

you. Then we'll be coming at 'em from three sides."

"That's about what I planned, all right," Holden said. "It's not far to the edge of town, you can see that from here."

"Then we'll move out as soon as that baggageman brings me my rifle," Longarm agreed. "You have any idea how far up the road Calder was going?"

"We figured he'd have time to walk about two miles."

"Then I'll go—" Longarm broke off as the baggageman came up carrying his Winchester. After he'd taken the gun, he went on, "I'll go about a mile before I hole up."

Side by side, the two men walked up the rutted road. A ten-minute walk took them to the last row of Brigham City's houses, and Holden pointed to a stand of dense brush a dozen yards off the road.

"That's about the best cover I'm going to find," he said. "I don't guess you'll mind making the rest of the way by yourself, will you?"

"Not a bit. I'll pace myself so I can be about midway between you and Calder, and settle down till they pass. Only don't look for me to show myself before we've got them fellows sorted out, so we won't be shooting at each other."

Holden nodded and started for the brush. Longarm kept walking up the road, cradling his Winchester in the crook of his elbow.

Chapter 4

As he walked down the rutted road—more a trail than a real road, he thought—Longarm glanced back now and then to be sure that he would be able to locate the spot Holden had selected for a hiding place. The thread of road wound like the loose end of a rope, twisting along the spine of a sparsely wooded spur of the Wasatch Range, which rose to the east. In the hard, dry soil vegetation had a hard job of rooting, and most of the growth was thin brush, barely as high as a man's waist.

After he had been walking steadily for half an hour by his guess, Longarm spotted a stand of scrub cedar ahead. It stood about twenty or thirty feet off the road, which dropped into a little hollow just beyond the brushlike trees. Stopping in his tracks, Longarm studied the clump of vegetation. Sweeping his eyes over the scant portion of the trail ahead, he decided that the cedar clump was about the best he could hope for in the way of cover. Turning off the road, he started toward it.

Though the stand of cedars was small and the tops of the stunted little trees barely reached above his head, they bushed out near the ground. Longarm found that when he hunkered down and leaned back on his boot heels the branches would hide him from someone passing by on the road. He pushed between the overlapping branches of the largest trees near the edge of the clump and settled down to wait.

Time ticked away slowly, but in his years as a lawman Longarm had spent untold hours in similar situations and he had long ago learned to be patient. He fished a cigar out of his vest pocket and lighted it, waving his hand in front of his face each time he exhaled to dissipate the smoke and keep it from rising above the tops of the cedars and disclosing his presence.

He had smoked the long, thin cheroot down to a stub and was getting ready to grind out the coal under his boot heel when he heard the distant scrape of horses' hooves ascending the sloping road beyond his hiding place. Moving unhurriedly, but wasting neither time nor motions, Longarm finished extinguishing his cigar butt and changed his position to be ready to move when the riders got closer.

Peering through the foliage of the cedars, he could see the riders as they topped the rise and moved toward him. Both had the look of hardcases. The westward-slanting sun caught them in profile, and Longarm could see that they both needed shaves. Both men wore the clothing favored by ranch hands —blue shirt and dun-hued jeans—and the garments of both were travel-stained.

One of the horsemen had a broad face, fat but not soft. It was marked now with trickles of sweat running down his cheeks and leaving trails in the dust that covered it. His eyes were almost hidden by folds of fat, and a knob of chin protruded from a neck almost as big around as his head.

His companion was lanky, and rode hunched forward in his saddle. By its appearance, his nose had been broken more than once. Between his high cheekbones its bridge was flattened and had two sharp twists above its thick flaring nostrils. A bushy moustache underlined the already prominent nose, its tips running down to bracket both sides of his full lips and taper off at the bottom of his protruding chin.

They had gotten opposite Longarm's hiding place and were about to pass by when a shot broke the early afternoon stillness and a man's voice rang out from the hump over which the horsemen had just ridden.

"Pull up, you two!" the speaker commanded. "And get your hands over your heads, or the next time I pull trigger I'll blow you outa your saddles!"

Instead of obeying the order, the riders reacted with the speed and practiced skill of men accustomed to meeting such sudden challenges. They reined their horses off the road, one

31

on either side of the narrow rutted path. Their boot heels thudded rhythmically as they pounded them into the animals' flanks, kicking them into a gallop.

Longarm stood up, raising his rifle. The horse ridden by the outlaw coming toward him had picked up speed instantly. Remembering what Holden had told him about the need to capture both bandits alive, Longarm took the horse as his target. Not wanting to kill the animal, he dropped the muzzle of his rifle, took aim at the horse's flailing hooves, and squeezed the trigger. There was no report, just the click of the hammer on an empty chamber.

Responding to the discipline he had trained himself to follow until it had become an instinct, Longarm let the rifle stock drop from his shoulder and swept his right hand to his Colt. His first shot kicked up dust, but he corrected his arm as the beast shied away from the revolver's crimson muzzle-blast and its loud report. Longarm's second shot hit its target, the off-hind foot of the shying horse. The animal neighed shrilly and started limping.

Its rider had drawn his pistol by this time. Longarm dropped flat as he saw the bandit raise his weapon. Before Longarm could bring his revolver to bear in his new position, the fugitive got off two quick shots. Both were high. The slugs whistled harmlessly through the cedar stand above Longarm's prone form and thunked the hard soil beyond it.

Now Longarm heard shots from the far side of the trail, the direction taken by the second outlaw. He registered the gunfire in his mind, but paid no other attention to it, for the man on the slanting ground beyond the thicket had grabbed his rifle from its scabbard on the limping horse and was running down the slope to an area of thick brush fifty yards away.

Knowing that at that range he was risking a chance of hitting the outlaw with a shot that would put him out of action without killing him, Longarm held his fire. The fugitive dived into the thicket and disappeared.

Anticipating his adversary's next move, Longarm dropped flat again. He reached the ground just in time. From the brush where the fugitive had taken cover, two rifle shots blasted and the slugs whistled their menace as they cut through the tops of the cedars above the spot where Longarm lay flattened out. Longarm was busy by then. The minute he had hit the dirt he had grabbed a handful of shells from his capacious coat pocket and was loading his Winchester.

You sure played the fool that time, old son, he told himself as his fingers worked with the skill of long experience. *You oughta been bright enough to check this rifle. If you'd had as much brains as a constipated jackass you'd've figured out that the railroad would've had a rule against letting a gun stay loaded in one of their baggage cars!*

While he was working, Longarm heard the sharp staccato of rifle fire sounding again from the direction taken by the other outlaw. This time he could make out the reports of three weapons in the gunshots: the sharp crack of a medium-calibre Winchester or Remington, the high bark of a Spencer carbine, and the dull, rolling thud of an old heavy Sharps.

Sounds like them two local marshals has got together and pinned down that other outlaw, old son, Longarm told himself silently as he finished shoving shells into the Winchester's magazine and pumped a live round into the chamber. *Between the two of 'em they oughta get him in hand pretty quick. And now that you're ready to go to work again, it's up to you to handle that one holed up over yonder.*

Longarm loosed an experimental shot from the Winchester at the brush where he had seen the fugitive take cover. He fired low, aiming at the hard soil at the edge of the little thicket, the slug kicking up the dirt and sending it showering into the heavy growth. The instant he had triggered off the round, a fresh peppering of wide-spaced shots came from the area where the two town marshals were closing in on the second fugitive. Counting on the distant shots to distract the outlaw in front of him, Longarm broke cover.

Bending low, he came out of the cedar stand at a run, and when no shot cracked as he emerged from the low, bushy trees he took off at a long slant down the slope. When he had covered fifteen or twenty paces with his quick, loping strides, Longarm changed his course and ran straight down the incline. The light scraping of his boot soles on the hard ground was the only noise he made as he picked up speed on the downslope. When he was well beyond the brush-clump where the outlaw had taken cover, he dropped flat, his rifle poised and ready.

Longarm did not have to wait long enough to question the effectiveness of his strategy. Only a moment after he had reached the position he'd been planning to take, the tops of the brush clump where his quarry had taken cover began trembling. Then the outlaw's feet broke from the cover of the thicket as he started backing out of his hiding place.

His legs followed, and his torso. In just a few moments he was out of the bushes, lying flat, still facing the low growth where he'd been holed up. Only then did Longarm learn that the man was the fat outlaw.

When the fugitive's slow, cautious backward wriggling had cleared his head from the brush, he rose to his knees. Raising his rifle, he peered for a moment over the top of the bushes that had hidden him, staring fixedly at the cedars where Longarm had been concealed. Without looking behind him, obviously convinced that Longarm was still holed up in the cedar stand, the outlaw dropped to his hands and knees and began crawling backward down the slope, keeping his eyes fixed on the cedars, his rifle muzzle pointing in their direction.

Longarm froze. He held himself motionless until the fugitive was only a dozen yards away from him, then got quietly to his feet and brought the muzzle of his Winchester around to cover the retreating outlaw.

"Stop right where you're at!" Longarm barked, his voice cold. "If you make a move I don't tell you to, you're dead!"

Without turning his head, the fugitive obeyed. His arms were extended above his head, one hand still grasping the stock of his rifle.

"You don't have to shoot me!" he gasped. "I guess I know when to give up!"

"That might be the first smart thing you've said in a long time," Longarm told him, his voice still icy. "Now, let go of that rifle. Move real slow, if you want to keep that hand you're holding it with."

34

His finger still on the Winchester trigger, Longarm kept his eyes fixed on the outlaw's hand as the man released the rifle stock and stretched his arm out away from the gun.

"Roll over on your back now and unbuckle that gunbelt," Longarm went on. "Soon as it's loosened, you can stand up."

Still obedient, his chubby face fixed in a scowl of concentration, the fat outlaw unbuckled his gunbelt and, after a moment of hesitation, sat up.

Longarm asked, "Which one are you? Wright or Weatherell?"

"Weatherell," the fat man replied unthinkingly. Then the implication of Longarm's question registered. A puzzled frown growing on his chubby face, he asked, "How in hell did you know our names?"

"You oughta be smart enough to figure that out," Longarm told him. "It didn't take long for somebody down in Colorado to put names to you and your partners right after the three of you held up that C&S train."

"But that was a long way from here!" the outlaw protested.

"Not long enough," Longarm replied. "Soon as your names got on the telegraph wire, you was as good as finished. Seeing as how the three of you didn't have sense enough to split up, the marshal up in Corrine pinned the right names onto you the minute you showed up in his town."

"That damn telegraph!" Weatherell moaned. "Seems like it don't matter much how fast a man moves anymore. Wherever he shows up, the word's already got there first." Then his face brightened and he went on. "Well, it looks like you caught me, but I guess Gene's got away free and clear."

"Don't count on it," Longarm said unsympathetically as he pulled handcuffs from the back of his belt and started securing them around his prisoner's wrists. "I got a hunch he's been corraled too by now." He locked handcuffs and went on, "All right. You can stand up and start walking."

As Longarm had anticipated, Jim Holden and Pete Calder were waiting on the road with their prisoner. Longarm shoved the fat outlaw to the side of his companion in crime.

"Now you got a pair in your hands," he told them. "With the one that got shot up in Corrine, that makes three of a kind,

35

which oughta cash in as a pretty good pot."

"Jim told me about you while we were waiting," Calder said. "He says there's some sort of law that keeps federal marshals from taking any kind of reward money."

"He told you a fact," Longarm agreed. "But it don't bother me none. You men are welcome to it."

"It sure doesn't seem right for you to be cut out," Holden said. "Isn't there something we can do for you that'll make up for all the trouble you've taken to help us?"

Longarm glanced at the sun, low in the western sky by now. He said, "Well, my train won't pass through Brigham City till noon tomorrow and until I get off it in Oakland about three days from now, this'll be the last chance I'll have to get a good night's sleep without being bounced and rattled awake half the night. If you was to steer me to whichever one of your hotels has got the best beds, I'd be right obliged."

"We can do a little better than that," Holden told him. "You're going to be the guest of Brigham City for the best supper the town can buy you and a room with a decent bed. Now, let's get these outlaws moving. I've got a pair of nice tight jail cells just waiting for them."

Longarm had stationed himself on the depot platform the following day and was waiting when the baggage car door opened and the baggagemaster began tossing suitcases and parcels through its wide door to the station's baggage clerk. When the clerk had taken the last pieces from the car and picked up the three or four pieces of luggage waiting to be placed aboard, he followed the man into the baggage car.

"Wait a minute, now!" the baggagemaster protested. "If you've got a ticket to get on this train, you've got to show it to the conductor before you can come aboard!"

"Oh, I got my ticket, and it's all in order," Longarm replied. He showed the man the continuation ticket given him by the conductor the previous day. "But I got a rifle with me, too, and this railroad's put in some kind of fool rule now that I got to check it with you till I get off."

"That's right," the baggagemaster nodded. "Too many

dudes from the East got to shooting at ranch cattle, taking 'em for buffalo. But the conductor'd bring your rifle up here when he saw to carry it aboard."

"That's what the conductor on yesterday's train done, and he damn near got me killed by taking the shells out and forgetting to tell me he'd unloaded it," Longarm replied tartly. "Now, if I let that happen once, I figure it ain't my fault. If I let it happen a second time, I'm a damn fool that ain't fit to hold the job I got."

"Just who are you, anyhow?" the baggagemaster frowned as the blast of the locomotive's whistle filled the baggage car and the train began moving.

"My name's Long. Custis Long, deputy United States marshal outa the Denver office."

"Well, that's a different matter, Marshal Long," the baggagemaster said quickly. "It's nice of you to take the trouble to bring your rifle back here yourself."

"Now, I took the shells out of the magazine and I got 'em in my pocket," Longarm went on. "If I need that gun, chances are I ain't going to have no time to waste. You better show me where you'll be putting it."

"We've got a regular rack for rifles at the back end of the car," the railroader said. "I can't break operating rules and neither can the conductor, so you can't carry it into one of the coaches with you, but I'll guarantee you'll have it real fast if you happen to need it."

"You won't need to worry about getting that Winchester to me if I should happen to need it before we get to Oakland," Longarm promised. "Now that I know where it is, I'll get it myself a sight faster than you can deliver it."

With a nod to the baggagemaster, Longarm started toward the back of the train. The Limited had picked up speed by now, and the clicks of the rail joints were sounding in a fast staccato as he made his way down the aisles of the swaying coaches.

There were no vacant seats in the first two passenger cars, and as he glanced down the aisle when he entered the third car, Longarm saw that it was almost as full as the others had been. He started down the aisle and covered almost half its length before he noticed the familiar face of a woman. She was staring at him in open consternation from one of the seats near the rear of the coach. Longarm stopped in his tracks and stared for a moment, unwilling or unable to believe his eyes. The woman staring at him was Ellie Benson.

Chapter 5

Keeping Ellie's eyes locked with his, Longarm walked slowly toward her. She was in a window seat, and the seat beside her was occupied by a chubby, red-faced man.

Stopping in the aisle of the swaying coach, Longarm leaned over the man and said quietly, "I guess we're going to have to have another little talk, Ellie."

"I don't suppose there's any way to avoid it," she replied, the tone of her voice telling Longarm that she was reluctant, but saw no way to refuse. She inclined her head toward her seatmate and went on, "I'd rather we talked someplace where we can be private, though."

"Sure," Longarm nodded. "Why don't you come along with me? The conductor on these trains has always got some little cubbyhole of an office fixed up back in the observation car. I imagine he'd let us set in there for a few minutes."

Ellie stood up and squeezed past the knees of the fat man in the aisle seat. Longarm stepped back to let her go ahead of him and they walked without speaking through the remaining coaches until they reached the observation car.

Five or six feet beyond the vestibule door, a ceiling-high partition had been built between the car's aisle and its outside wall. The cubbyhole formed by the wall was closed with a heavy curtain. Longarm knocked on the edge of the partition. The curtain was pulled aside and the conductor stared at them for a moment. He'd taken off his uniform cap and a heavy red line running around his forehead showed where it had rested. He frowned as he looked from Longarm to Ellie.

"I know you, ma'am," he said to Ellie. "Window seat three, car four, ticketed through to Oakland." Then he turned to Longarm. "Who the devil are you, mister? And what're you doing on my train? You must've gotten on at Brigham City, but I sure didn't punch your ticket."

"I don't reckon you did," Longarm replied. "I got aboard on the baggage car. I wanted to leave my rifle there." He took his continuation ticket from his vest pocket and offered it to the trainman. "Here's my ticket, if you want to punch it."

Glancing at the ticket, the trainman nodded and said, "It looks all right. Is that why you came back here, just to get it punched?"

"That wasn't exactly what I had in mind, but—"

"It's got to be done sooner or later," the trainman interrupted. "Hand it here. I might as well take care of it now." He took out his pocket punch and closed its jaws over Longarm's ticket. As he handed the strip of cardboard back to Longarm, he asked, "Now, what's that you said about getting on at the baggage car to leave your rifle? I'm supposed to check any firearms that are brought onto this train, mister. If you were trying to smuggle a loaded weapon aboard—"

Longarm broke in on the conductor. "I wasn't. I don't need to. My name's Long, deputy United States marshal outa Denver." He took out his wallet and flipped it open to show his badge. "If you want to go up to the baggage coach and take a look at my rifle, you're welcome to do it, but I had something in mind besides getting my ticket punched when I come back here."

"What's that?"

"Me and this lady need to have a little private talk, and your cubby here is the only place that come to my mind."

"You're not arresting her, are you?" the conductor's eyebrows drew together as he turned his gaze on Ellie. "Because if I've got criminals on my train, I want to know about it!"

"Now, just simmer down," Longarm said quickly. "I ain't arresting her. All I want is a place where we won't be bothered while we're talking."

"Well, I suppose I can let you use my office," the conductor said slowly. "I haven't walked the train since we pulled out of Brigham City. That'll take me fifteen or twenty minutes. Is that enough time for you?"

Longarm nodded. "It oughta be. I'm much obliged for your help."

"Just don't disturb my paperwork," the conductor said as he picked up his cap and settled it in place. "Other than that, you can make yourselves right at home."

Longarm held the curtain back while Ellie slid into the bench seat. Then he let the heavy fabric drop and folded his long legs to sit opposite her.

"Well, Ellie," he said, "maybe you better start out by telling me why you changed your mind about going back to Denver, like you promised me you would."

For a long moment, Ellie sat silent, her head bowed to avoid meeting Longarm's eyes. He waited patiently. Then to give him a reason for breaking his scrutiny, he took out a cigar and lighted it. For some reason he couldn't fathom, Longarm's movement triggered Ellie to reply.

"I just didn't feel comfortable going back to Denver, Longarm. All I could think about was making that nasty little killer you're going after pay for murdering Jed."

"I take it you had it in mind to shoot him?"

Ellie nodded silently, her eyes downcast now.

Longarm went on, "Even after you'd promised me you'd let the law take care of the Stovespit Kid?"

With a sigh, Ellie nodded. "Even after that," she agreed. "It's not that I don't trust you and Billy Vail, Longarm. I guess I've just got this feeling that it's up to me to avenge Jed's murder."

"So you got off the train to Denver someplace—Laramie or Cheyenne, most likely—after I'd put you on it. And then you got on this one, figuring I was outa your way," he nodded.

"It was Laramie," Ellie told him. "And it didn't enter my mind that you'd be anyplace but on your way to Oakland. You weren't supposed to be on this train any more than you were on the other one. You're the last person I expected to see."

"Everybody's plans get spoiled now and again, Ellie," Longarm observed. "Not that it makes that much never mind, but I wasn't looking to see you again on this trip, either."

"I suppose you're going to put me off, then, and start me back to Denver again?"

"Well, I'll admit that's in my mind. Except after what you done before, I'd suspect you might try the same trick again."

"I'm not sure I wouldn't," Ellie admitted.

"Jed lived by the law, Ellie," Longarm reminded her. "Why can't you do the same thing?"

"This is the first time I've ever thought about doing anything else, Longarm," she said slowly. "But every time it pops into my mind that the man who murdered my husband is still alive himself, I guess I just sort of go a little bit crazy."

"Was I to put you on a train going back to Denver again, what do you suppose you'd do, Ellie?" Longarm asked. "Pull the same stunt of doubling back?"

"I just don't know, Longarm," Ellie replied. "If you want the plain truth, I didn't really plan to try to catch up with you this time. It just . . . well, it just seemed to happen, like somebody was telling me to get off in Laramie and try to get to the Stovespit Kid before you could start back to Denver with him."

"You know what would happen if you gunned him down."

"Oh, of course. I'd be arrested and I'd have to stand trial for murder. I'm not a fool, Longarm, and I know you aren't, either. Even if you testified against me in court, do you think a jury would bring back a hanging sentence?"

Longarm considered Ellie's question briefly, then shook his head. "No. No, I don't imagine they would, seeing you was just getting back at the man that murdered your husband. Likely you'd get put in prison for a while, but I don't suppose you'd hang."

"I could stand going to prison if I got my revenge."

"Now, hold on!" Longarm protested. "The way you're talking now, I got the idea you still expect to keep on trying!"

"Of course I do!" she told him firmly. "Regardless of what you try to do to stop me. Sooner or later, I intend to shoot the Stovespit Kid."

Longarm made no reply for several moments. Then he said sadly, "I reckon you know that you ain't leaving me much of a

42

choice. Even if I ain't got much stomach for it, I'll have to arrest you."

"Go ahead," Ellie invited. She extended her arms, holding her wrists together. "Go on, Longarm. Put me in handcuffs!"

"Now you're being silly!" Longarm snapped. "But since I can't get you to promise to settle down and wait while the law takes care of the Stovespit Kid, I'm going to fix things up so you can't get close to him while we're in Oakland."

"You mean that you're going to put me in jail?"

"That ain't what I said, Ellie," Longarm protested. "When I was out in California on a case a while back, I made friends with the head detective of the Southern Pacific's railroad police. I'm going to ask him to look after you while I go see about the Stovespit Kid. After I figure out what the best thing to do is, I'll let you know."

"That was sure a nice meal you treated me to, Chief Edwards," Longarm said as they mounted to steps of the squat stone building that housed the Oakland police department and city jail. "I wouldn't mind eating at that Dalkey's place again, but I'm due to start back with the Stovespit Kid tomorrow, if we can get all the paperwork done before the eastbound Limited pulls out in the morning."

Matt Edwards, chief of the Oakland police department, was a husky man who wore the harried frown common to so many ranking policemen. He had insisted on taking Longarm to Dalkey's Saloon for a beer and a supper of the establishment's corned beef and cabbage free lunch before they worked out the formalities of the Stovespit Kid's transfer and signed the necessary papers.

"Well, he's down in one of the holdover cells in the basement, unless he's pulled one of his escape tricks," Edwards said. "Do you want to see him before we start writing up the transfer papers?"

"Not especially. There ain't no reason why I should, is there?"

"There's no law that says you have to," Edwards answered. "As I told you while we were having supper, he was safe in

43

his cell when the shifts changed at six o'clock. But unless you do things differently in your jurisdiction, it's usually customary for an officer picking up a prisoner to take a look at the man before we do the paperwork. That leaves both of us sure we're talking about the same prisoner."

"Well, I wouldn't want you to change your routine on my account," Longarm said. "I don't mind looking at him, if that's the way you generally operate."

"I'd feel better if you did," the police chief nodded. "It won't take much time. You can identify him, I suppose?"

"I got a look at him once before, in Denver. I didn't like what I seen, and I sure ain't planning to enjoy having to be stuck with him for the next four days. I guess I can put up with it, but there's one other thing I need to talk to you about."

"You're referring to the woman you told me about while we were eating supper?"

"That's right. Ellie Benson."

"Let's take first things first," Edwards suggested. "We'll go take a look at the Stovespit Kid, then come back to my office and talk about the woman."

"Lead the way," Longarm said. "Now that we've got to talking about him, I'm sorta curious to hear what he's got to say for himself."

"Come on, we'll go downstairs. I've had him kept in an inside basement cell. With the Stovespit Kid's reputation, that was the safest place I could think of."

Longarm followed the chief down a corridor to a short flight of stairs. They entered a brick-walled room, its only light a gas jet fixed in the center of the ceiling. There were four cells in the enclosure, and three of them were unoccupied, their doors ajar. The fourth seemed vacant, too, but its door was closed. When Longarm looked closely at the cell's solitary bunk, he could see that the humped tangle of blankets on the bunk concealed a man's prone form.

"Wake up, Mahoney!" Chief Edwards called. "Marshal Long's here to take you back to Denver, and he wants to take a look at you."

"Let the son of a bitch come back tomorrow," a nasal voice

44

snarled from the bunk. "I got to look at so many horses' asses during the day that I don't want to have to look at night, too."

"You need to learn how to mind your manners, Mahoney," Longarm said quietly. "Maybe I can give you a few lessons on our way back to Denver."

"Aw, shit!" the man under the blankets growled. "I never saw anybody with a badge on who knew anything about manners."

Hardening his voice, Longarm said, "I'll give you just two seconds to get your head out so I can see your face. If you don't move, I'll come in there and move you!"

"Well, I'll be damned if you don't sound like you're really one of the tough ones," the prisoner said. As he spoke he sat up and let the blanket drop away.

Although Longarm had seen several Wanted posters with artist's sketches of Chauncey Mahoney, alias the Stovespit Kid, he was not prepared for the Kid in the flesh.

Mahoney's face was fish-belly white. His brows were thick and beetling, his nose a shapeless blob that looked as pasty as his face. His lips were thick and blubbery, his chin grotesquely elongated, and when he twisted his face into a scowl as he gazed through the bars at Longarm and Edwards, he showed a ragged set of snaggled teeth, two of the upper ones missing.

"All right," Mahoney sneered. "Take a look at me, if you've got to. Better make it a good one. I might not be here later on. I've got better things to do than go back to Denver."

Exercising a good deal of restraint, Longarm did not reply. Instead he turned to Edwards and said, "One look is all I need. I'll see more'n I want to of him on the way back."

Edwards nodded and led the way to the stairs. As they walked down the corridor he said, "I don't know about you, but that fellow Mahoney's about the nastiest piece of work I've ever run across."

"You said what I was thinking," Longarm replied. "I sure don't relish listening to him yammer away at me on the way back to Denver, but it's part of the job I do."

Edwards led the way into his office. Settling down at his desk, he motioned for Longarm to take a chair across from him. While Longarm was lighting a cigar, the chief suggested, "I thought it'd save you time if we do the paperwork on Mahoney now. All your extradition papers seem to be in order."

"That suits me," Longarm nodded through a cloud of blue cigar smoke. "I'll come by and pick him up in time to catch the eastbound Limited in the morning. When I'm riding herd on a slippery son of a bitch like the Stovespit Kid, I don't aim to waste any time delivering him."

"We've had him in our holdover cell for a week or more now," Edwards frowned. "So far, he hasn't done anything to justify his reputation for making slick getaways. But, just to be safe, I ordered my men to tell me immediately if he even *looked* like he was planning a getaway."

"That don't mean he ain't been figuring up a way to give me the slip," Longarm replied. "He's had plenty of time to think about making the trip back to Denver, and knowing he's due for a walk up them steps to put on a rope necktie oughta have stirred his brain up quite considerably."

"I suppose it has," Edwards nodded. "And I'll be glad for you to take him off our hands, Longarm—Marshal Long," he corrected himself. "I don't think I know you well enough to—"

"Don't get fussed up about my nickname, Chief," Longarm smiled. "I answer to it better'n I do to my right name."

"It's just the other way around with me," Edwards said. "I haven't held down this job long enough to get used to being called 'chief.' My friends call me Matt."

"Let's be friends, then, Matt," Longarm suggested. "And I didn't say that just because I'm going to need a friend to handle that little extra piece of work I mentioned to you while we was having supper."

"You're talking about that Mrs. Benson the SP is holding in jail for you on your temporary custody request?"

Longarm nodded. "Handing her over to the SP railroad police at the depot was one of the hardest jobs I ever had to face, Matt. I don't want to see Ellie hurt or harmed or do something that'd get her in trouble. Her husband was the closest I ever come to having a partner."

"It seems to me she's better off with you protecting her,"

Edwards said. "If she carried out the threats you mentioned and killed the Stovespit Kid in my jurisdiction, I'd have to hold her on a murder charge."

"Sure," Longarm agreed. "But all the same, I feel real bad about it."

"What do we do now?" Edwards frowned. "You can't leave her with the railroad police, and if I take temporary custody of her I can't hold her very long. Sooner or later, she'll have to be brought to trial or released. You know that, Longarm."

"Sure. And I been thinking about what to do. How long do you figure you can hold her without getting yourself in trouble?"

"A week at the most."

"That ain't such a hell of a long time," Longarm said. "It's going to take me four days just to get the Kid back to Denver. Then there's the paperwork Billy Vail's clerk will have to do getting him indicted, and after that we still got to wait till the judge gets his case on the docket."

Edwards said thoughtfully, "If you were to file another charge, I suppose I could stretch it another week or so."

"If I was to swear out another charge, could you stretch it as long as two weeks? That'd give me time to see if I can get the Stovespit Kid's murder case started. Ellie's going to have to be a witness when he's tried."

"What kind of charge do you have in mind?" Edwards asked.

"All I can come up with is for me to file on her for harassing a law officer. I don't know if there's a law like that out here in California, but it's the best I can do."

"That ought to be good for another week or two," the chief nodded. "It'll take that long for the city attorney to find out whether there is such a charge in California, and I can stall a few more days before she is released."

"Well, to keep your record clear, all you got to say is that I asked you to hold her till I can arrange her transportation back to Denver. Then I'll pull down the charge and you can let her go free."

"I don't see anything wrong with that," Edwards agreed.

"We'll leave it there, then," Longarm said. "Now, if you got all them forms filled out, I guess we can get 'em signed."

"I'll sign them first, then pass them over to you," Edwards told Longarm, reaching for the pen that stood in its holder beside the ink bottle. "Technically, you're supposed to take custody of a prisoner at once after these are signed, but I don't see that a few hours' delay will make any difference."

For the next few minutes, the only sound in the office was the scratching of pen on paper as Edwards signed the sheaf of transfer documents. He passed the pen to Longarm and pushed the ink bottle closer.

"Soon as I get through putting my signature on these, I guess I better get over to my hotel," Longarm said, as he dipped the pen in the inkwell. "It'll be good to sleep in a real bed instead of propped up in a railroad—" He stopped short as the door to Edwards's office flew open and a uniformed policeman burst in.

"Excuse me, Chief," he gasped. "But the sergeant said I was to tell you right away. That prisoner in the holdover, the one they call the Stovespit Kid—he's just got away!"

Chapter 6

Longarm and Chief Edwards both jumped to their feet.

"That's impossible!" Edwards exclaimed. "Marshall Long and I were both down in the holdover until just a few minutes ago."

"It sure ain't been more'n three or four minutes," Longarm agreed. "How in hell did he manage to move so fast?"

"Well, I couldn't answer that, Marshal," the policeman said. "All I know is that he's gone and his cell's empty."

"Who found he was gone, and exactly when?" Edwards asked.

"Sergeant Mulcahy went to the locker room to get some cigars out of his coat pocket about two minutes ago," the policeman replied. "He came running back upstairs and told me to find you and tell you the Stovespit Kid wasn't in his cell."

"Let's go, Matt!" Longarm urged. "The quicker we get after that slippery son of a bitch, the easier he's going to be to find!"

"Don't be in too big a hurry," Edwards said. "For all we know right now, he might still be in the building, holed up in a closet or a storeroom or even on the roof." He turned to the policeman who had brought the news of the escape. "Where's the sergeant now?"

"He stayed at the desk," the officer replied. "I was just coming out of the file room when he got back from the locker."

"Go tell Mulcahy to pull all the men he can together and start searching the building," Edwards ordered. "I don't care whether they're on duty or off. Tell them not to overlook anything: storage closets, file room, lockers, the whole place."

"Yes, sir, Chief!" the policeman said.

When the officer had left at a fast walk, Edwards turned back to Longarm and said, "The best thing we can do right now is to stay here in headquarters until we're sure the Stovespit Kid hasn't just holed up in a closet or one of the rooms that isn't used during the night."

"He ain't had time to cover very much ground, that's for sure," Longarm nodded. "But supposing he's outside, where's the likeliest place he'd head for?"

"That'd depend on how well he knows Oakland." Edwards frowned. "My guess is that if he knows anything about the Bay Area he'll do his damnedest to get to the waterfront."

"And head for San Francisco?"

"I'd lay a bet that that he'll try to get across the Bay sooner or later," Edwards nodded. "He's got a bigger town to hide in, and once he gets to the Barbary Coast he'll find plenty of people who'll help him hide. He won't have that here. The nearest thing we've got to a criminal element on this side of the Bay is concentrated along the dock area."

"I've been down to the Barbary Coast," Longarm said. "I got to agree with you, it's where I'd head was I on the run from the law. It won't take five minutes for the Stovespit Kid to hole up, once he gets there."

"Well, if he's hidden on this side of the Bay, we'll dig him out fast. My men know the area a lot better than the Stovespit Kid would, since he's a stranger here."

"What if he heads inland?" Longarm frowned.

Edwards shook his head. "I doubt he'd try it. There's no place for him to hide in that direction. Oh, a couple of little towns, but it's mostly farms and a few orchards. After you get across the little hump of the Coast Range foothills, it's just flat farmland until you hit the delta country."

"I guess I'd have to put in with you on the way you figure," Longarm said. "If your men don't pull him out of a hidey-hole, it's a pretty sure bet he's gone to San Francisco."

"He'd more than likely have that in mind. It'd be easier for

50

him to hole up there than anywhere else close. I'm sure you know that gangs like the Sydney Ducks and Black Hand and the Chinese Tongs were doing business in San Francisco when Oakland wasn't anything but a big stretch of mud flats. Gangs never really got rooted on this side of the Bay, so we don't have much trouble with them."

"But from what little I know about him, the Stovespit Kid's a loner. He wouldn't belong to a gang."

"Any crook that's ever operated in California knows enough to make a beeline for the Barbary Coast when he needs a place to hide from the law, Longarm."

"Well, that's true enough," Longarm agreed. "But the Kid ain't been free long enough for him to get to San Francisco, or much of anyplace else."

"Oh, I'm not overlooking that. What I'm hoping we can do now is keep him from getting there. If he's still on this side of the Bay, my men will find him."

"Well, it's your town, Matt," Longarm said. "So you call the tune, and I'll dance right along."

Before Edwards could reply, the policeman who had brought the news of the Stovespit Kid's escape came back into the office. "Sergeant Mulcahy's down in the assembly room, Chief," he said. "He'd like for you to come down here, if you're not too busy. He says he's got something you oughta see."

"Let's go, Longarm," Edwards said. "He might've found something that'll set us on the Stovespit Kid's trail."

Mulcahy, a rotund man whose rosy face might have served as a map of Ireland, was standing at one side of the large room. Its only furnishings were several rows of benches, and all four of its walls were lined with high, narrow wooden doors. Several of these were open or ajar, and the sergeant stood in front of one of them, a heap of rumpled clothing on the floor at his feet.

"This is how that damn prisoner got out without anybody noticing him," he said to Edwards, indicating the bundled garments. "This is Lanson's locker. He's on daytime duty right now, and he always changes into his uniform here at the station."

Edwards nodded. "That means the Stovespit Kid just waited until the coast was clear, then put on Lanson's uniform and walked out right under our noses."

"There's always somebody coming and going around here," Mulcahy protested. "When we're busy at the desk, we don't have time to inspect everybody who comes in or goes out."

"Calm down, Mulcahy!" Edwards said. "Nobody's blaming you or anyone else. Right now, the main thing is to get the Stovespit Kid back."

Longarm had hunkered down beside the clothes while Edwards and the sergeant were talking. After he had pawed through them, he picked up a pair of dungarees and held them up for Edwards to look at.

"Your sergeant's right, Matt," he told the chief. "These sure looks like the pants the Kid had on when you and me was talking to him."

"They probably are," Edwards agreed. He turned back to Mulcahy and went on, "What I want to know is how that slippery son of a bitch managed to break out of his cell."

"I think I can answer that, Matt," Longarm said. He rose to his feet and held out a piece of twisted metal for Edwards and the sergeant to inspect. "This was in the pocket of the pants."

Edwards took the metal object and looked at it, a frown growing on his face. It was a teaspoon, its handle bent into the shape of an L and twisted at an odd angle.

While he was turning the spoon around in his fingers, Longarm asked, "Don't you make a count of your eating tools after you've fed your prisoners in the lockup?"

"Of course we do. That's a routine procedure, a standing order," he replied.

"Well, somebody must've been sitting down." Longarm grinned lopsidedly as he spoke. "Because if you was to try this spoon handle on the lock of your cell, I'd bet dollars to doughnuts you'll find it unlocks that door."

"That's my guess, too," Mulcahy put in before Edwards could speak. "One of the jailers must've gotten careless."

"I'll have somebody's hide for this!" Edwards gritted.

Then he asked Mulcahy, "I hope that's all the bad news you've got for me?"

"Yes, sir. Of course, I'll get started right away on finding out if anybody noticed the prisoner going out of the building."

"Don't waste your time," Edwards told him wearily. "With his cell empty and a uniform missing, we can be pretty sure that he got away without being noticed."

"Looks like it's about time for you and me to hit the street and see if we can find him," Longarm suggested. "Even if all we got was a quick look, you'd notice right away that he wasn't one of your men."

"That's about the one advantage we've got, I suppose. Let's go, then. We'll start looking for the Kid right now. If we're lucky, we can get him back before he's gone for good."

"I guess you know all the men on your force pretty good, Matt," Longarm said as they got into the buggy and Edward slapped the reins over the horse's back.

"Why, of course I do! That goes with the job."

"What I'm getting at is, if we was to see the Stovespit Kid you'd know right off that he wasn't one of your fellows, even if he's wearing one of your uniforms."

"I'd spot him in a minute," Edwards replied. "Even in the dark. That's why I'm going to zigzag around on our way to the ferry. We've only got four beats between headquarters and the most direct way to the ferry slip. We might see one or two of the patrolmen and tell them to be on the lookout for the Kid."

"You know your town," Longarm said. "Go ahead and do whatever you think is best."

For the next quarter of an hour the two men rode silently as the buggy wheeled in a zigzag course through the dark streets. They encountered only one of the Oakland policemen, and he had seen nothing of their quarry. When they came in sight of the night-black water of the Bay, Edwards reined up in front of the ferry slip, which was empty now, and he and Longarm alighted.

"Let's take a look through the windows before we go into the waiting room," the police chief suggested, indicating the squat square building in front of them. "We don't know whether the Kid got here in time to catch the last boat, but if he didn't he might just be brassy enough to go inside and wait."

"Well, I don't figure he'd be likely to do that kind of a fool stunt, but it's worth a try," Longarm agreed.

He followed Edwards to the nearest window and they stood peering through its grimy pane for a moment. There were only half a dozen people waiting for the next boat, and none of the men had on a police uniform.

"If I was in the Stovespit Kid's place, I'd be too smart to wait in there," Longarm observed as they turned away from the window. "I'd find me a hidey-hole out here on the ferry slip, someplace where it's dark, and jump aboard at the last minute."

"I'm sure that's what the Kid did," Edwards agreed. "Chances are he didn't even go inside. We might be wasting our time, but let's go inside and find out. The clerk ought to remember if he saw a man in one of our uniforms getting on that last boat."

"No, sir, I haven't seen any of your men tonight, Chief," the ticket clerk said in reply to Edward's question. "If the fellow you're looking for did get on the last boat that left, it's just about nosing into the San Francisco slip now. The only way to find out is to wait till it gets here on its next trip."

"That won't be for another half-hour," Edwards told Longarm. "Then, by the time you get across to the San Francisco, the Stovespit Kid will more than likely be holed up somewhere."

"Do you reckon we better do some more looking around here?" Longarm asked. "We ain't even sure yet that the Kid took the ferry. He might still be someplace close by."

"There's a chance he is, but I don't think it's a very good one." Edwards frowned. "You're right about doing some more looking, though. We can cover the beats between here and headquarters before that ferryboat gets back, and we'll be waiting when it pulls in."

For the next quarter of an hour, Longarm and Edwards

rode in a zigzag pattern around the waterfront. They peered into dark corners and alleyways, checked warehouses and sheds, and in the course of their search ran across two of the patrolmen on duty. Neither of the men had seen anyone wearing a police uniform, and none of the corners they explored yielded any trace of the escaped prisoner.

"He's bound to have left on that ferryboat," Longarm said at last. "But I got to be sure before I go after him. Maybe we better head back to the slip."

"I was thinking pretty much the same thing," Edwards nodded. "The quicker you find out whether the Kid crossed on that ferry, the sooner you can get on his trail."

When they returned to the slip, the ferryboat was just nosing in toward shore. Longarm and Edwards were waiting when the slip hand cranked down the gangplank, and they jumped to the deck of the vessel before the passengers began hurrying off. As they shouldered their way through the disembarking passengers, the mate of the ferryboat came to meet them.

"Evening, Chief." The man nodded to Edwards. "You mind telling me what's happening? You and your friend was in as big a hurry to get on as that policeman of yours was on our last run. The way he acted gave me the idea there's some kind of trouble. What's going on?"

"That man you took for one of my patrolmen was an escaped prisoner," Edwards replied. "The uniform he had on is one he stole from the station. We're trying to run him to earth."

"Well, I'll be damned!" the mate exclaimed. "I thought he was about the ugliest and sloppiest policeman I ever seen, but it didn't occur to me he might be running away from you."

"You didn't have no reason to've thought something like that," Longarm said. "And I don't suppose you paid any special mind to him."

"Not beyond noticing how ugly he was. That was when I seen him shoving up to the bow, where he'd be first to get off."

"Did you notice which way he went when he left the ferry?"

"There wasn't much way for him to go except out through the regular gate. But I didn't actually see him go out. I was too busy with my regular jobs to pay attention."

"Well, thanks for the information," Edwards told him. He turned to Longarm and went on, "I suppose you'll just stay on the boat and start looking for the Kid across the bay?"

"I don't see how I can do that, Matt," Longarm frowned.

"You'll want to hit his trail while it's still hot, won't you?"

"Sure. But it won't cool off all that much in an hour or so. Besides, I want to be legal when I go after him."

Edwards looked at Longarm, his brows knitted into a frown. "I guess I don't follow you. You're an officer of the law in pursuit of a fugitive. What could be more legal than that?"

"If you'll recall, the Stovespit Kid's still your prisoner, Matt," Longarm replied. "I was just getting ready to sign the papers transferring custody to me when your man busted in to tell us he'd flew the coop."

"I'm not going to let red tape stand in your way, Longarm," Edwards said. "We can finish that paperwork any time after you catch up with him."

"That might not be real soon," Longarm replied. "And it might even be that I'll have to follow him someplace else when I get on his trail again. Besides, even if you and me had wound up deciding what to do about Ellie, I feel like it's due her for me to break the news that she's going to have to be locked up here in Oakland for a while."

"I can understand that." She's your old friend's widow and you feel you owe it to her," Edwards said. A long blast of the vessel's whistle drowned his next words, and when the sound died away he went on, "I see your point, all right. There's no way of knowing where you might have to go when and if you pick up the Kid's trail. We'd better get off the boat right now."

"That's what I was thinking," Longarm agreed. "I figure it'll be close to an hour before the ferry gets back on its next trip. That oughta be plenty of time to unwind the red tape, and I want to see Ellie safe in your holdover before I leave."

"Well, that's no problem," Edwards said as they started down the pier. "We're just a little way from the railroad police office. We'll pick her up and take her with us."

"If it's all the same to you, Matt, I'll take one of the hacks that's waiting at the end of the wharf and go pick her up by myself. I'd like to have a minute to talk to her before I hand her over to you."

"Whatever you say. I'll be waiting when you get to head-quarters."

In the hackney cab taking them to police headquarters, Long-arm told Ellie, "Now, I ain't got no choice but to put you in what we call protective custody. And I'm certain you know what that means. I'd guess you heard Jed talk about it more'n once."

"Oh, I know what you're talking about, all right!" Ellie snapped angrily. "Protective custody means you can keep me locked up until it suits you to let me go. I'd rather you arrested me!" She extended her arms to him again. "Go ahead, put your handcuffs on me."

"Handcuffing you never even crossed my mind. I don't figure you're going to jump outa the hack while it's moving."

"I suppose you're going to take me and the Stovespit Kid to Denver, then?" Ellie asked, her voice artificially sweet. "You can't watch both of us every minute, Longarm, and it won't matter how hard you try to stop me, I'll find a way to kill him."

"Oh, I been giving that some thought, too," Longarm told her, holding back his still-aroused anger at her stubbornness. "I've fixed it up to leave you here. The Oakland police chief's going to put you in a holdover cell, so you're going to be safe while I take care of the Stovespit Kid."

"You see!" Ellie smiled triumphantly. "You are going to put me in jail, even if you deny it."

"A holdover cell ain't the same thing as being in jail, Ellie," Longarm said, exercising all of his considerable will-power to keep from getting angrier than he was already.

"I've seen holdover cells," she said. "When I was trying to learn how to be a good wife to a lawman, right after we got married, Jed took me into more than one jail to show me around. I could see right away that any jail cell's a cell, no matter what you might call it."

"Just the same, you're going to be in a holdover until I get the Stovespit Kid safe back to Denver," Longarm promised. "Then I'll wire the Oakland police chief and tell him to let you go."

"But that means I'll be locked up for at least a week!" she protested.

"About that," Longarm agreed.

Ellie suddenly changed her tactics. Her voice no longer angry, but soft and pleading, she asked, "How can you do this to me, as good friends as you and Jed were?"

"You didn't have to ask me that, Ellie," Longarm replied.

"I did, though," she said, a taunt in her voice.

"I'd rather walk ten miles barefoot over hot coals than to see you locked up behind bars," Longarm went on. "But you ain't leaving me any other way to go. And all you got to do . . ." He stopped and shook his head.

"Go on," Ellie invited, after she'd waited a moment for him to continue. "What is it I've got to do?"

"You know what it is as well as I do. Get over this idea of revenging Jed's murder. Trouble is, the way you been acting, I ain't too sure I can depend on anything you might promise me."

"Suppose I really promise to stay away from the Stovespit Kid?" she suggested. "And I mean really and truly this time, Longarm."

For a moment Longarm stared at Ellie fixedly. Then he shook his head sadly.

"No," he told her, his voice low but firm. "There ain't no use in us hashing this thing over any longer, Ellie. I ain't going to let you stand trial on a murder charge. You're going to be locked up in that holdover in the Oakland jail till I've got the Stovespit Kid to Denver and put him away behind bars where you can't get at him."

Chapter 7

A cold, wet fog was settling down over San Francisco Bay by the time Longarm got back to the Oakland ferry slip. The smoke from the long thin cigar he'd lighted after getting in the hack at police headquarters curled blue from the cigar's tip, mingled with the mist, and was lost as he walked toward the landing. Even before he reached the slip, the running lights of the approaching ferryboat broke through the haze that hung over the night-black water of the bay.

Buttoning his long coat in a vain attempt to shut out the raw chill, Longarm watched the vessel as it slid into the slip and the dockwallopers rushed to throw mooring lines aboard. Only a handful of passengers stood in the ferry's prow and as yet none of the San Francisco-bound people in the waiting room had come out. When the ferry's steam whistle broke the night's stillness and the incoming passengers started disembarking, those who had been watching in the waiting room began straggling out.

They crowded up against Longarm, pushing him into the center of the small opposing surges of landing and departing passengers. He found himself being jostled on all sides as he walked onto the boat, looking for the deckhand he and Edwards had talked with earlier. He spotted the man standing beside the cabin door and went over to him.

"If you're going to have a few minutes after we get started across the Bay, I'd like to talk to you again," Longarm said.

"After we get outa the slip, I don't have a lot to do until we get across," the man replied. "But I don't know that I could tell you any more'n I did when I talked to you and Chief Edwards on our last turnaround."

"Maybe not, but it's been a while since I was in San Francisco, and I need to find out how much it's changed since I was there last time."

"Whatever you say, Marshal," the deckhand nodded. "I'll be glad to help you any way I can. But with this fog settling in, I got to stand lookout in the bow, so it's going to be cold and windy."

Cold and windy didn't tell half the story, Longarm decided when he joined the deckhand in the bow of the ferryboat shortly after it left the slip. The fog grew thicker as the ferryboat's paddlewheel propelled it toward the San Francisco side of the Bay, and though the breeze hadn't increased, the boat's motion created its own wind. The icy air crept around Longarm's upturned coat collar and trickled down from his neck to his chest and torso in icy streams, while from the top of his boots to the crotch of his trousers the chill cut through the legs of his longjohns and formed goosebumps on his thighs.

"I been a lot warmer cutting across a prairie in the face of a blue norther than I am right now," he remarked as he joined the deckhand in the vessel's prow. "And I ain't going to stay out here any longer'n I got to."

"Go ahead and ask me what you want to know," the ferryman said. "Then you can get back to the cabin and warm up."

"Mainly I need to find out what things are like now in San Francisco," Longarm went on. "It ain't that I'm a stranger to the town, but it's been a while since I visited there last. I was wondering if the Barbary Coast's changed much."

"Hell, it'd take an earthquake to change it!" the deckhand replied. "The old district's still just where it's been as long as I can remember, and I'd imagine it'll be in the same place a long time after you and me are dead and gone."

"As I recall, the middle of it was just about on Pacific, between Broadway and Kearny," Longarm said.

"You might find it's spread out some, if it's been a long time since you was there, but you called the turn just about right. What's left of the Sydney Ducks still hang out in their old stamping grounds, only there ain't as many of 'em as there used to be. And the Chinks has took over damn near everything along Grant and Stockton. But you won't find all that much of a difference."

60

"Now, it seems to me like I recall that there used to be a lot of cheapjack stores right beyond where the ferry puts in, across the Embarcadero, along Battery and Clay," Longarm went on. "I guess they'd still be there?"

"You might find a few more than there used to be," the ferryman replied. "But if it's old clothes you're looking for, you can sure get 'em. And I guess you'd remember that if you go on a little farther from the waterfront you can find just about anything else that anybody wants."

"Well, from what you've said, I don't reckon I'm going to be too bad off when it comes to finding my way around," Longarm told the man. "And I thank you kindly for your help. Now I'm going to go set in the cabin. My toes is just about froze, and I need to get 'em warmed up."

There was little warmth in the cabin, but by the time the boat had docked Longarm's feet had begun to tingle as warmth came back to them, and he took long strides as he walked slantwise across the broad expanse of the Embarcadero and turned into Clay Street. The cheapjack stores that he remembered from his past visits were still crowded close together, and a majority of them had lanterns hanging over their doors and were lighted inside inspite of the late hour.

Most of them occupied narrow wooden buildings, and all of them displayed every conceivable kind of used clothing, from sailors' oilskins to the faded uniforms of long-dead fraternal orders. A few had shelves or racks of clothing in front of their establishments, but most of them showed their wares simply by hanging the garments on nails driven into the walls. Longarm entered the first of the stores and found the proprietor busy sorting coats from a heap that took up most of the floor.

"I'm looking for a policeman's suit," he said. "Wonder if you might have one?"

"A policeman uniform I don't have, mister. You vant any other kind, maybe I can fix you up. A nice one from the Sons of Erin, maybe? Or the United States Cavalry? Maybe a navy officer's good blue suit, you take off the brass buttons, you got a fine set business clothes."

"All I'm interested in is a policeman's outfit," Longarm

replied. "Guess I'll just have to keep looking."

With minor variations he repeated the same conversation in the next three stores he tried. In the fourth, he picked up a trail.

"A policeman suit, yet? Hah! Just tonight I didn't buy vun! Could maybe I show you something else?"

Longarm shook his head. "It ain't the suit I'm looking for. I'm after the man that sold it."

"So," the proprietor nodded. "He stole it from you, yet?"

"Not from me, but he stole it all right," Longarm replied.

"You are maybe a detective, then?"

"I'm a deputy U.S. marshal. I'm looking for the man who stole that policeman's outfit, and it sounds to me like you remember him."

"So qvick I should forget such a face?" The storekeeper shook his head. "So ugly!"

"It sounds like that's my man," Longarm nodded. "I don't reckon you seen where he went after he left here?"

"From such a thief I should take my eyes off, yet? He vent across the street." Turning to the door, the man pointed to the store on the other side of the narrow thoroughfare. "Go talk to Mordecai. And don't let him put you off. A trade he made with the ugly one."

"Thanks," Longarm said. "You been real helpful."

By the time he had crossed the narrow street, Longarm had his next move planned. He wasted no time in preliminaries when he entered the shop, but showed his badge to the man who came to greet him.

"You'd be Mordecai," he said abruptly. "And you've got some information I need."

"So I'm Mordecai," the man shrugged. "But from information, I don't know vat you mean."

"A little while ago this evening, you swapped some clothes with a man who stole a policeman's uniform," Longarm went on. "Now, I ain't here to make trouble for you, but I want you to tell me what that fellow had on when he walked away."

"Trouble I don't need, Officer," Mordecai said quickly, his eyes still on the badge in Longarm's hand. "You vant the policeman suit, go on, take it. It ain't like something I can sell fast."

"I'm after the man, not the suit. All I want you to do is tell me what you swapped him for it."

"A pair of pants vith a coat." The proprietor shrugged.

"What color were they?

"Brown duck pants," Mordecai replied. This time, the shrug was in the tone of his voice. "The coat, grey wool. So they don't match, but a policeman's uniform, who's going to buy?"

"Thanks," Longarm nodded. "Now one more thing. Which way did that fellow go when he left here?"

"Down Clay Street, toward Portsmouth Square."

"You been real helpful, and I thank you," Longarm said, turning to leave. "I won't bother you no more."

"Vait yet, mister! The police uniform, you vant it back?"

"It ain't my uniform," Longarm answered. "It belongs to a policeman over in Oakland. I can't be bothered toting it with me, but you might hold on to it. I got an idea the officer it was stole from will come get it after he finds out where it is."

Leaving Mordecai staring speechlessly after him, Longarm left the shop. *Well, old son,* he told himself as he touched a match to a fresh cheroot, *you know the Stovespit Kid's likely to be holed up somewhere here on the Barbary Coast. Question is, which one of these places is it? There's a lot of 'em along the streets, and maybe twice as many as shows, places crooks know about that honest folks don't even know are here.*

He continued walking down Clay until he reached Montgómery Street, then turned north. The character of his surroundings changed rapidly now. The cross streets were narrower here and were spaced closer together, some of them little more than brick-paved alleys. Whether street or alley, all the thoroughfares were crowded with buildings that had more imposing fronts than the cheapjack shops nearer the waterfront, but were jammed against one another even more closely.

Lanterns were not used for lighting in the fringes of the Barbary Coast where Longarm began his search. On the facades of most of the buildings large acetylene lamps were fixed, most of them tilted upward, to cast the greatest part of their light on the signs above the doors while leaving the actual entryway in obscurity, illuminated only by the gleam that came from the lamps inside. In further contrast to the almost-deserted waterfront streets, these streets were crowded.

Longarm walked slowly, zigzagging from one side of the narrow street to the other rather than trying to bump his way along the narrow, busy sidewalk. He scanned the faces at the bars in saloons bearing such names as the Eagle, the Lion's Head, the Hawksbeak, the Moose, the Arizona, the Montana, the Lone Star, the Buckeye, the Louisiana, the Thunderbolt, the Occidental, the Magpie, and a score of others.

Wise enough in the ways of fugitives to take his time, Longarm pushed his way to the entrance of each saloon along the streets he covered. On the Barbary Coast, doors were not popular in drinking dives, but Longarm's height allowed him to peer over the tops of those which had batwings, and when he came to those that were doorless he had a clear view of the interior.

A glance usually told him what he needed to know. He paid little attention to the more pretentious places where the drinkers were businessmen wearing suits and derby hats, and where the saloon girls were young and attractive in their thigh-length skirts and low-cut bodices. When he looked into a saloon whose patrons were clad in dungarees and wore tattered cloth caps and battered boots, and where the bar girls ranged from tired-looking middle-aged women to raddled hags, he scanned the face of every man lined up at the bar.

Longarm was not only looking for the ugly face of the Stovespit Kid. Though the Kid was his real quarry, Longarm had little hope of finding him so easily. He realized that the Kid was too cunning to show himself openly, but reason also told him that since law breakers from all over the West took refuge on the Barbary Coast, the odds were very good that he would recognize some other law breaker who could be persuaded to reveal the most likely places where a man on the run might be found.

Working as methodically as the cut-up maze of narrow

streets and narrower alleys allowed, Longarm moved steadily along. He had reached Pacific after groping through a maze of nameless alleys where the only light was the glow of red lanterns in the windows of tiny weatherbeaten shacks.

After the unpaved alleys through which he had been groping, Longarm felt better with a brick sidewalk under his feet. He stopped a few paces from the corner to light a cigar while he studied the brighter lights gleaming ahead of him on both sides of Pacific. His cheroot was drawing now, and Longarm started toward the lights, a blue-grey trail of tobacco smoke whirling behind him in the faint night breeze before it merged with the thin fog.

He was still a dozen yards away from the rectangle of light that streamed through the doorless entrance of the saloon when the light was blotted out momentarily by a shapeless running form. A shot rang out from the saloon and the blurred moving figure stumbled, almost falling. A second shot sounded and as the dark silhouetted form moved and rose and started running toward him, Longarm could see that the outlined shape was that of a woman.

Again the light from the doorway was blotted momentarily as a man came out. Even at the distance that separated them, Longarm saw the sheen of blued steel glistening from the barrel of a stubby revolver as the man raised his hand.

Reacting instinctively, Longarm began his draw before the silhouetted man could level his weapon. The Colt barked, its muzzle-flash brightened the night, and though the man in the saloon doorway got off his shot, the heavy slug from Longarm's Colt had gone home before his finger closed on the trigger.

As the silhouetted man crumpled and fell, his gun spoke, but the bullet screeched harmlessly along the brick sidewalk. The woman had reached Longarm by now. She threw herself at him, and he caught her as she lurched forward.

"You hurt?" Longarm asked.

"A little bit," she gasped. "His first shot creased my leg. But I can still move. Will you help me get away from here? His friends will be after me right away!"

"Sure." Longarm juggled his Colt for a moment as he took

the lighted cigar from his mouth and ground its glowing tip out under his boot heel. "Which way do you want to go?"

"Let's cross the street. If we can make it to Montgomery before they get after me, we'll be all right."

Holding the woman with his strong arm around her waist, Longarm started at a slant across Pacific Avenue. They had reached the darkness that shrouded the mouths of the alleys from which he had just emerged before he heard footsteps thudding on the brick pavement behind him, and were now in the deep shadows that hung over the mouths of the alleyways.

Longarm could hear the voices of the two men who had come from the saloon. They were swearing at the darkness to which their eyes had not yet adjusted. Putting on a final burst of speed, Longarm and the limping woman reached the corner of Montgomery Street and turned into its sheltering darkness before their pursuers from the saloon spotted them.

"There's a doorway just a few steps ahead," she said. "We can hide in it. If they don't see us, they'll more than likely think I've ducked into one of the alleys."

A moment later, she indicated the wide, dark doorway of a darkened cut-stone house. Longarm helped her into its shelter and they settled down on the steps. They sat silent, listening, but heard neither the voices nor the footsteps of the men who had been pursuing them.

"Looks like we shook 'em off," Longarm said, his voice low. "If they'd spotted us turning up the street, they'd be here by now."

"I think you're right," she agreed. "Neither one of them's very smart."

"If you know who they are, you'll know who the fellow was that I knocked down," Longarm told her. "Now maybe you better tell me what all the shooting's about."

"I can't," she said. "But I've got to take care of this scratch on my leg as soon as I can. If you'll just take my word that it's all right, and help me get home, I'll be glad to pay you almost anything you ask. I don't have any money with me, but if you'll believe me—"

"Hold on," Longarm broke in. "I don't know anything about you. I don't know your name, what you're up to, or why."

"I'm sorry, but I can't explain," she replied. "But I can tell you one thing, you won't be getting on the wrong side of the law if you help me."

For a moment, Longarm was silent. Then he asked, "Are you trying to tell me you're some kind of law officer?"

"Not exactly. But I am on the right side of the law, even if that might be hard for you to understand, the way things happened back there."

Longarm recognized the ring of sincerity in her words. He said, "I got a hunch you're telling me the truth."

"I certainly am!" she said emphatically. "Even if I can't tell you anything to back up my situation."

"Then I'll tell you something that might change your mind and make you feel better, too. My name's Custis Long. I'm a deputy United States marshal outa the Denver office, and I'm here on a real messed-up case. Now, if what you been telling me is the truth, you don't have no reason to hold back anything from me."

"I hope you can back up what you said."

"Sure I can." Longarm fished into the inside breast pocket of his coat and produced his wallet. "I don't know as you can see my badge, dark as it is—"

"Then strike a match. I've got to be sure," she said.

"I'll just kill two birds with one stone," he told her.

Taking out a fresh cigar, he clamped it between his teeth, struck a match, and lighted it, then held the match over the badge. His companion leaned forward to look at it, Longarm got an impression of red hair, blue eyes, and high cheekbones while she studied the badge. Then the match burned short and he flicked it away.

"I think that must be the prettiest badge I ever saw," she sighed. "I don't have a badge, but I'm on the side of the law. My name is Jennie McCoy. I'm working for what's left of the Committee of Vigilance. We're trying to get enough evidence to put Abe Ruef in prison."

"Maybe you better tell me who this Abe Ruef is," Longarm suggested.

"Being from Denver, I don't suppose you've heard about him. Abe Ruef is the political boss of San Francisco right now. He's a slimy crook, but he's got a tight hold on the city government, and he's responsible for making the Barbary Coast what it is. If we can get enough evidence to put him in the penitentiary, we can make San Francisco a decent place again."

"Well, I've heard about your committee," Longarm said. "I guess what you are is sort of a spy for them?"

"That's as good a description as any," Jennie replied. "But my leg's beginning to hurt me, Marshal Long. My flat's just a little way from here. If you'll help me home, I'll fix us a cup of hot coffee, and maybe there's something about that messed-up case of yours that I can help you with."

"You know, I got a halfway hunch you're right," Longarm said. "It might just be you're the one who can set me on the track I ain't been able to find yet. But what about that fellow I shot? Hadn't we ought to find a policeman—"

"That's the last thing you'd want to do!" Jennie exclaimed. "That was one of Ruef's men you shot. The policeman would just hand you over to the gang and you'd never be heard from again!"

"You mean the gangs and the police are in cahoots?"

"Of course. How else could the Barbary Coast exist? Please do as I ask. If you still don't believe me when we've talked things over, you can always go to police headquarters and tell them you shot that fellow. But right now, the safest place for both of us is where I want you to take me."

Longarm's instinct told him that what Jennie said was true. "All right," he replied. "Just tell me which way to go, and I'll make sure we get there."

Chapter 8

"Go right on in, Marshal Long," Jennie McCoy said.

She opened the door of her apartment and motioned for him to enter. The room beyond the door was dark, and the memory of past ambushes caused Longarm to hesitate for a moment before he moved. Jennie brushed past him and he heard vague fumbling noises across the room, then the rasping of a match. He blinked when it flared up. She held the burning match high and touched its flame to one of the gas jets that protruded from the wall. When it spurted light, Jennie adjusted the flame and lowered the etched glass shade over the jet, then turned to face Longarm.

"I'll start a pot of coffee," she went on. "Then we can settle down in comfort and talk about our cases."

Jennie moved to the second lamp and lighted it. Longarm remained standing by the doorway, taking his first really good look at her.

Jennie was a tall girl, but was so well-proportioned that she did not seem to be outsized. Her scanty costume left little to the imagination. She wore an abbreviated blue satin dress over a pair of flesh-colored tights. The skirt's hem came only halfway down her thighs and the bodice was low-cut, emphasizing the fullness of her bulging breasts. Her face was elongated, but it went well with her height. Her jaw was firm, her mouth generous between a firm chin and a Roman nose. Her red hair was now in disarray above her high brow. Her eyes were ice-blue, sparkling in the gaslight.

"Would you mind closing the door?" she asked. "It has a spring lock, so all you have to do is pull it shut." Then she smiled and added, "If you're wondering, I haven't any secrets or hidden traps planted to surprise you."

"I didn't have anything like that in mind," Longarm told her as he closed the door, "but I was thinking that I might be butting in on something you was intending to do."

"I'd intended to spend most of the night in that saloon, but Ruef's plug-ugly spoiled that plan. And remember, it wasn't your idea to come here, it was mine," Jennie reminded him. "Please sit down and make yourself comfortable. I don't keep any liquor on hand, so I can't offer you a drink, but I'll start some coffee brewing just as soon as I do something about this bullet crease in my leg."

Longarm's eyes followed the gesture of Jennie's hands and he saw the brownish-red stain of drying blood on the outside of her right thigh, a handspan above her knees. The stain was not a large one, and the dark line in its center where a scab was forming was less than half the width of a finger.

"If you need for me to do something, just let me know," he said. "I've had plenty of experience with bullet creases."

"Lord bless you, so have I," she smiled. "My father was a small land-holder in Ireland, and I've two older brothers who followed him when the troubles started. I was the oldest girl, and my mother couldn't stand the sight of blood, so I had to do all the family bandaging before father got wise and emigrated."

"That little crease you got don't really look bad enough to need a bandage," Longarm told her. "It's already drying up."

"Just the same, I'll take a good look at it before I start the coffee brewing. And then we'll have a chance to talk. Sit down, now. I'll be back before you finish your cigar."

Longarm selected the most comfortable of the four chairs in the small square room and began inspecting his surroundings. The room was as bare and impersonal as any he had ever seen. The furnishings were sparse and simple: a small divan and a square table on opposite walls, and three chairs in addition to the one he occupied. The room had no decorations or pictures, no mementos or souvenirs. His cigar had been half-smoked even before they got to Jennie's flat, and by the time she returned he had puffed it down to a stub.

"I'll get you a saucer for your cigar butt," she told him.

She turned and disappeared for a moment, returned carrying a saucer, and handed it to Longarm, saying, "Not that dropping some ashes on the floor would hurt this threadbare carpet. Thank goodness I can get away from this place now and then and go home."

"You mean you don't really live here?"

"No. I've got a flat over on Russian Hill," Jennie replied as she settled down on the sofa. "But I sleep here about half the time, when I'm tired or the weather's bad and I don't feel like going home. This place is rented by the Committee, a sort of field headquarters."

"I had the idea that the Vigilance Committee went out of business quite a while ago," Longarm frowned.

"Officially, it doesn't exist," she said. "But a few years ago, when Abe Ruef came out of the woodwork and started trying to take over the town, a few members of the old Committee got together quietly and began working to stop Ruef."

"That's the second time you've mentioned this fellow Ruef. I never heard of him myself, but of course I don't get to San Francisco all that often. Who is he, and what's he doing?"

"He's a little jackleg lawyer, or was in the beginning. If you remember, Marshal Long, the old Committee of Vigilance cleaned up the Barbary Coast pretty well, but that was quite a while ago. The Committee thought the job was finished, and disbanded. Things did stay quiet for a while, but little by little the thugs and thieves and swindlers and pimps and gamblers came back, and after a while they were doing business just about like they had before."

"So these men you're working for now put the Vigilance Committee back together," Longarm said.

"Yes, but they kept quiet about it this time."

"And they hired you to be a spy down here? You're digging up evidence against this fellow Ruef and his gang?"

"Exactly," Jennie nodded. "Of course, I'm not the only one working on the job. I don't know who the others are, and I don't suppose they know any more about me than I do about them."

"I'd guess you write down whatever you've found out and mail it to some post-office box, then?"

"Oh, no. I write reports and leave them on that table over there, but I never see whoever comes and gets them. And every few days, I'll find a note on the table, telling me to stay away from here on a certain day. When I get one of those notes, I go home to my own flat and rest."

By this time the fragrant odor of brewing coffee was drifting into the room. Longarm inhaled it and said, "That coffee smells like it's just about ready to drink, Jennie. And I could sure use some. I been moving around pretty smart-like since supper time."

"I'll get some for both of us. Why don't you take off your coat, Marshal Long? You'll be more comfortable. I suppose you know we're going to have to stay holed up here for a while, until the fuss over that shooting has settled."

"I figured we'd have to do that," Longarm replied.

He rose and slipped his arms out of his coatsleeves, then draped the coat over the back of a chair while Jennie returned to the kitchen. She came back carrying two cups of coffee and put them on the table, then settled down into a chair. Longarm pulled a chair up to the table for himself and sat down, taking out a fresh cigar.

"Now, then," he said, after lighting his cheroot, "maybe I better start by telling you about this case of mine."

Using as few words as possible, he described the Stovespit Kid, sketched the details of how he'd been captured and escaped from the Oakland jail, then summed up his own pursuit of the Kid to the time when he'd picked up the fugitive's trail earlier in the night.

"So I figure he's holed up here someplace on the Barbary Coast," he concluded. "But this ain't my kind of territory, and I don't know anything about where to look. If you got any ideas, I'd sure be glad to listen to 'em."

"I'm a long way from knowing all the hideouts myself, Marshal Long," Jennie admitted. "I've uncovered about forty, but I'm sure there must be three times that many."

"Well, I sure don't aim to go back to Denver without him," Longarm said. "Forty or four hundred, it's all the same to me. But since we're going to be in this thing together, you might as well drop that 'marshal' business. Just about everybody I know calls me Longarm, and I answer to it better'n I do to anything else."

"Longarm," Jennie smiled. "The long arm of the law, of course." Her smile became a thoughtful frown as she went on, "There are a lot of crooks here on the Barbary Coast, but there aren't too many who fit the description of this Stovespit Kid, as you call him. I have an idea that if I do a little nosing around I'll be able to get a line on him."

"I'd sure be grateful if you can. That Stovespit Kid is a real slippery character, and if I let him get too far ahead of me, he might slip plumb away from me again."

"It wouldn't be a good idea for me to show myself in any of the dives tonight," Jennie went on thoughtfully. "I'm so tall that people have a way of remembering me. But tomorrow I'll change clothes and put on the blond wig I wear when I go out during the day. Then I can walk around and ask some questions."

"Looks like I better head back down toward the middle of town and find me a room in a hotel," Longarm said. "Where do you want me to meet you tomorrow?"

Jennie hesitated for a moment, then said, "I don't see any need for you to go all the way back to Market Street, Longarm. I'm afraid my sofa's too short for you, but if you don't mind a hard bed, I can fix you a pallet."

"Now, that's real thoughtful of you, Jennie. If you're sure it won't be putting you to a lot of trouble—"

"It's just common sense," Jennie broke in. "It'll save both of us a lot of time. I've got two thick quilts I don't use at all. I'll just make a pallet of them, and that'll be that."

Moving with swift efficiency, Jennie brought the quilts from her bedroom. She laid one on the floor and folded it lengthwise for a mattress, then spread the other over it for a cover.

"That sure looks good to me," Longarm told her. "I been sleeping on a train for the better part of a week, and it'll feel real nice to sleep on something that ain't going to jounce me around all night."

"Good night, then," Jennie said. She started for the door of her bedroom, stopped, and looked over her shoulder. "Don't worry about breakfast. I'll fix us something when we get up in the morning."

Longarm wasted no time undressing. He stripped down to his balbriggans and laid his Colt on the floor where it would be within easy reach of his hand. The gaslights were only half a step away. He turned them out and groped for the pallet with his bare toes, found it, and slid under the top quilt. Almost a full twenty-four hours had passed since he'd slept last, and the hours since then had been busy ones. Within a minute, he was sound asleep.

Longarm had no idea how much time had passed before a noise roused him. His gun hand went unerringly to the butt of his Colt, and he had it in his grip even before he was sitting up on his improvised bed.

There was no light in the windowless room, and all that he could make out were patches of greater and lesser darkness. Then, as his eyes adjusted to the gloom, he became aware that one of the areas at which he was staring was a bit less dark than the space around it. He closed his eyes, squeezing his eyelids tightly, and when he opened them he could see a bit more than before.

Jennie was standing in the open doorway of the adjoining room. A faint glow of light from her bedroom outlined her figure, and Longarm could see that she was naked.

"Is something wrong, Jennie?" Longarm asked.

"Yes, and I just realized what it was," she answered. "I went to sleep thinking about you, then all of a sudden I woke up all excited and realized I'd been dreaming of you. Please come to bed with me and make my dream come true, Longarm."

"I sure won't wait for you to ask me a second time," Longarm told her.

He levered himself to his feet, his Colt still in his hand, and a single long step took him to Jennie's side. She held her arms out and Longarm swept her into an embrace, bending to kiss her. Jennie's lips pursed as they kissed, drawing Longarm's tongue into her mouth, and her hand slid down to his crotch.

74

Though the shades on the twin windows of the room were drawn, enough light from the street outside filtered through and around the edges of the shades to create a bit of light in the room. Longarm could see Jennie's face when she looked up at him, her blue eyes glowing.

"Take me to bed, Longarm!" she gasped. "Hurry!"

Longarm needed no urging. He clasped Jennie around her slim waist and lifted her, reached the bed in one long stride, and lowered her onto it, dropping his Colt on the floor beside the bed as he bent down to find her lips again.

Jennie sprawled her thighs and guided his shaft, and when he felt her moist warmth closing around him, Longarm lunged. He drove in with a single swift thrust that brought a cry of ecstasy from Jennie and set her hips heaving in quick, frantic gyrations. He began stroking fast, and Jennie clasped her legs around his hips, pulling herself up to meet his drives.

Suddenly Jennie's straining body began trembling, and small sobbing sighs burst from her throat. Longarm read the signs and continued thrusting deeply in a regular rhythm until Jennie's back arched and a cry rose in her throat. She twisted frantically as Longarm kept driving. Then with a final, sharp scream she grew rigid and her body jerked while her screams reached a crescendo that faded into gasping, gusty breaths, and her tenseness gave way to utter relaxation.

Longarm was still far from being ready to stop. He slowed the tempo and intensity of his thrusts, and went into her now with slow, deliberate penetrations. Jennie lay limp and listless while Longarm continued.

He had maintained his slow stroking for several minutes before Jennie stirred again. She reached up and locked her fingers around the back of his head and pulled him down until their lips met again, and her tongue sought his. They held their kiss, tongues entwining, until a shudder swept through Jennie's body. She turned her head, breaking their kiss.

"Don't you ever get tired?" she asked in a whisper.

"Oh, sure. But I ain't tired yet. I'll quit if you want me to, though."

"Don't do anything of the kind!" she said quickly. "You're the first man I've ever known who can keep going this long,

75

and I'm not going to let go of you until you can't move any more!"

"I'll take my time, then."

"Do, Longarm. I want you to. But . . ." she hesitated.

"But what?" Longarm asked.

"Can you turn to put me on top without separating us?"

"Sure." Longarm clasped Jennie around the back and rolled until Jennie was above him. "How's this?"

"Just wonderful. Now just lie still and let me set the pace this time."

Jennie began slowly. She leaned forward, her arms stiff, while she turned and twisted her hips, moving slowly and deliberately, but keeping herself impaled on Longarm's rigid shaft until he was into her full length. Her round, soft breasts were bobbing above Longarm's face now, and he lifted his head to take one of her protruding tips in his mouth. He rasped his tongue over its pebbled surface, and Jennie responded by increasing the tempo of her hips' gyrations.

After he'd tongued one tip for a while, Longarm transferred his attention to the other. While he was caressing her breasts, Jennie kept grinding her hips, pressing firmly against him as she twisted her torso from side to side. Longarm looked up at her face. Her eyes were closed, her head thrown back, an ecstatic smile on her full lips. Some sixth sense must have told her that he was watching her, for she opened her eyes and looked down at him.

"I hope you're enjoying this as much as I am," she said.

"I'm doing fine," he told her. "Let go again if you feel like it. I can hold on for quite a while yet."

Jennie responded by speeding up the gyrations of her hips. After a few more of her wild twists, she threw back her head and bore down even harder on Longarm while she screamed as she shook through another spasm of ecstasy.

When her cries of joy became louder and closer together, Longarm was ready himself. He pounded even faster, and let his control go. Soon after Jennie's throaty cries merged into one loud ecstatic shriek, Longarm began jetting, pulling her close to him, holding her shuddering body until he was drained and his taut muscles relaxed. He sighed deeply, and released Jennie's hips. She collapsed on the rumpled bed and he dropped down to lie beside her.

For a few moments they lay quietly, in happy exhaustion. Then Jennie said, "Nobody's ever given me that much pleasure before, Longarm. If I wasn't so tired, I'd be ready to start from the beginning and do it all over again."

"Rest a while. Daybreak's still two or three hours away, and I can't think of a better way to spend the time."

"We've got more than two or three hours," she told him. "The Barbary Coast doesn't wake up with the chickens, Longarm. There's not a thing we can do about finding the Stovespit Kid until the middle of the morning."

"If we got all that much time, maybe we better doze for a little while. I don't need much sleep to freshen me up, so you rouse me whenever you feel like it."

Jennie raised up and bent over to kiss Longarm, the soft kiss of a happy but sleepy woman. Then she dropped her head to his shoulder and he pulled her close to him. In less than a minute, both of them were asleep.

Chapter 9

When Longarm heard the tiny clinking of metal striking metal he snapped awake instantly. Opening his eyes, he was surprised to find that daylight glowed through the drawn shades of the windows and that he was alone in the bed. Another small sound broke the flat's silence and he made two moves almost simultaneously: He came to his feet and he grabbed his revolver from the chair by the bed.

He stood still for a moment, listening, recalling that at some time during the night he'd been roused by a noise from outside the flat and had reached for the weapon only to have his hand close on empty air. He'd gotten up at once, being careful not to wake Jennie, and put the Colt in its accustomed place.

Now, with the room bathed in soft light filtering through the window shades, Longarm could see that he had been alone in the rumpled bed. He glanced around for his longjohns before recalling that he had taken them off in the living room the night before and left them lying on the pallet where he'd started his night's sleep. Holding the Colt ready, he padded on bare feet across the bedroom and stopped just inside the door, peering around the doorjamb.

Nothing moved. The living room was just as it had been the night before. The pallet on which he had started his night's sleep was just as he'd left it, his missing balbriggans in a heap on the top quilt. Still another noise reached him from the open door across the living room. Longarm crossed to the door and saw Jennie, fully dressed, in the flat's tiny kitchen. She was bending over the stove, where eggs and bacon were sizzling in a frying pan. The aroma of the bacon filled the room.

At that moment Jennie turned away from the stove. When she saw Longarm standing naked in the doorway with his Colt in his hand she began smiling and a chuckle broke from her lips. She said, "You don't need your gun to persuade me, Longarm. I'll go quietly back to the bedroom with you."

Longarm realized how he must look, and his smile matched hers. He said, "I got some habits I can't get rid of, Jennie. Being careful about risking my hide is one of them."

"You were sleeping so soundly when I woke up that I couldn't bear to disturb you."

"Now, that was a nice thought, Jennie, and I thank you kindly. I guess I was pretty wore-out last night."

"So was I," she said. "But when I woke up the first thing I thought of was that I didn't have anything we could eat for breakfast—or lunch, if you want to call it that. So I went out and bought some eggs and bacon."

"That bacon smells mighty tasty. And the eggs look good, too," Longarm said, coming up to the stove to stand beside her.

"I also brought back a bonus with them . . . one that should make you feel good."

"If I felt any better, I'd start singing, even if I can't carry a tune in a washtub. But why didn't you wake me up? I'd have been glad to take you to a café for breakfast."

"And if we'd gone to a café, I'd have missed the bonus."

"You've mentioned that bonus two times now, Jennie. Maybe you better ease my curiosity and tell me what it is."

"I will, but if I keep looking at you standing there naked, reminding me of last night, I'm going to drag you back to bed."

"You wouldn't have to do much dragging. I'd sorta like that myself. Come on."

"Not now, Longarm. I'm ready to dish up breakfast, and we can talk while we eat. Later on, we might not have much time for either talking or eating."

"I'll slip my pants on, then. I'm real interested in what that bonus you keep talking about is."

Jennie had their breakfast on the kitchen table when Longarm returned, dressed now except for his coat.

"Come on over to the table and sit down," she said. "I can tell you just as easily while we're eating."

After they had taken a few bites to ease the edge of their hunger, Jennie went on, "You were so sound asleep when I woke up that I didn't have the heart to disturb you, Longarm. I even took my clothes into the living room to dress. When I realized I'd have to go out to buy food for breakfast, I decided that I'd wait until I got back to wake you."

"That was a real nice thought, but I oughta got up and gone alone with you."

Jennie shook her head. "No, Longarm. The people I needed to talk with are used to me. I'm part of the Barbary Coast's landscape now. They wouldn't have said a word if you or any other stranger had been with me."

"What's all that got to do with this bonus you been teasing me about?"

Suddenly serious, Jennie said, "I'm not really sure it's a bonus yet. I just started calling it that because it might lead us to the Stovespit Kid."

"You ain't joshing me, are you?"

"That's something I wouldn't joke about."

"Now you really got my bump of curiosity swelling up, Jennie. Go ahead and tell me the rest of it."

"I don't know how much of what I stumbled over is anything more than hopeful. We're going to have to find that out later."

"Right now I'd settle for just about anything."

"From what you've said, you don't know the Barbary Coast very well," Jennie began.

"I've had to work it a time or two, on cases that brought me to San Francisco. But it's been a while since I was here."

"Did you ever run into a Mexican family named Ortega on any of your cases here?"

Frowning, Longarm shook his head. "If I did, I'd be pretty sure to remember. There just wasn't many Mexicans around the Barbary Coast when I was here before."

"There aren't too many now. Even the Ortegas don't live

close to the district, and they haven't been here very long."

"Maybe you better explain how they fit in, Jennie."

"I guess the best thing would be for me to start from the beginning." Jennie frowned. "The Ortegas own a little bakery and grocery store just few blocks from here, at the edge of North Beach. Their bakery makes the best sourdough bread in San Francisco, and I buy what food I need there when I'm going to fix a meal in the flat."

"But if they ain't mixed up with the Barbary Coast—" Longarm began.

Jennie interrupted him. "What I'm trying to tell you won't make sense until I finish, Longarm."

"Go ahead, then."

"When I went into Ortega's this morning, one of the girls from the Magpie was in there. She calls herself Nita, but she's only half-Mexican, and she doesn't speak much Spanish. I just happened to overhear her asking Ramon Ortega if he'd seen the ugly man she sent to the Ortega house yesterday."

"And that reminded you about the Stovespit Kid, I guess."

"Of course it did, after what you'd told me about him."

"Well, if there was a prize for ugly, he'd sure take it," Longarm nodded. "So I guess you started asking questions?"

"Not until I'd done some listening. I really hadn't been paying much attention to Nita until she mentioned the ugly man, but after I heard that I followed her when she went outside and asked her a few questions."

"I guess you got some answers, or you wouldn't be telling me about it."

"All I got was a few bits and pieces. I've tried to put them together, and I think I've figured out what must've happened. This ugly man that Nita was asking Ramon Ortega about showed up in the Magpie last night, and she got to talking with him. Of course, that's what she's supposed to do. I suppose he asked her where he could find a hole to hide in or how he could get away."

"Stands to reason," Longarm said when Jennie stopped to catch her breath. "San Francisco ain't the easiest place to make a getaway from. The ferry landings are easy to watch, and as I recall there's only two roads going south, down the peninsula."

"That's right," Jennie went on. "And what I didn't know until I talked to Nita this morning is that the Ortegas have a little steam launch that they use to deliver their sourdough bread to customers across the Bay and in the delta country and up in Marin County."

"And nobody'd be likely to think about looking for a man on the run to leave San Francisco that way," Longarm said slowly.

Jennie nodded. "From what you told me about the Stovespit Kid being so slippery and tricky, it struck me that it's the kind of trick he might pull."

"It looks to me like my next move is to see if I can pry something outa the Ortegas," Longarm said thoughtfully. "But I can't make out why they'd want to get wound up with crooks, since they got a good business going in their bakery."

"I can answer that for you," Jennie told him. "The Ortega family used to own a big ranch down the peninsula, south of San Francisco. It was one of those old Spanish land grants, with a lot of flaws in the title, and they got into a dispute with the state over its boundaries. Abe Ruef was their lawyer."

"And he helped 'em hang on to their ranch?"

"No. They kept a little bit of their land, but they lost a lot of it. But it was one of Abe Ruef's first big cases."

"That just might be the string that ties the whole thing together," Longarm said slowly. "They'd feel like they owed him for helping 'em, and he'd have some kind of hold over them."

"That's how it looks to me," Jennie agreed. "But there's one thing that still bothers me."

"What's that?"

"If the Ortegas helped the Stovespit Kid make a getaway, I'm sure they would make him pay for their help. If he's just escaped from jail in Oakland, how would he raise the money?"

"He's been a crook for a long time, Jennie, and a pretty smart one, if you can call any crook smart. He might've had some hidey-hole here in San Francisco where he tucked away money he'd stole before. That might be why he headed here. Or maybe he just went out and pulled a job to get what he'd need."

"I suppose he could've gotten enough money that way," she agreed. "I've found out that crooks here on the Barbary Coast often pull twenty or thirty robberies every night. That's one reason why the Committee of Vigilance came back to life."

"Whatever he done, I guess my next move is to go have a talk with this Ramon Ortega fellow."

"I'm ready whenever you are," she said.

Longarm shook his head. "No. From here on out, you got to steer clear of this case I'm on."

"But, Longarm, I—"

"Jennie," he broke in, "think about it a minute. If the Ortegas are still tied in with this Ruef fellow, and you go along with me to poke into their affairs, how long do you think it'd take for him to find out about it?"

"Not very long," she admitted. "A day or two at the most."

"And how long after that do you figure it'd take for Ruef's killers to run you down?"

"I've got to agree with you, Longarm," Jennie said. "But I'll sure miss you, even if we didn't have much time together."

"You're a real sweet girl, Jennie. I'll miss you, too, and I thank you for all the help you give me. But from here on, I got to handle this case by myself."

During the short walk from Jennie's flat to the Ortega's store in North Beach, Longarm mulled over the best way to persuade Ramon Ortega to talk. His final decision came quickly.

There ain't no use in beating around the bush, old son, he told himself. *Just take the bull by the horns and rassle him down to size.*

Ortega's store was a much larger establishment than Longarm had expected to see from Jennie's description. It occupied a large tin-front building that took up nearly the entire side of the short block of Kearny Street between Vallejo and Dunne's Alley. The store was almost empty of customers at that hour of the afternoon. Its cavernous interior was divided into four parts, one dealing in fresh produce, another in meats, a third in grocery staples, and the fourth in baked goods. Longarm went directly to the bakery section.

"I'm looking for Mr. Ramon Ortega," he told the aproned clerk who came up to the counter.

"He's in his office in the bake shop, but I'll be glad to call him for you."

"Never mind calling him," Longarm said. "Just show me where his office is."

"But Señor Ortega does not allow us to disturb him when he is in his office I cannot—"

Longarm took out his wallet and opened it to show his badge. He said, "I'm on official business, so just forget about what Mr. Ortega don't let you do, and show me where his office is."

For a moment the clerk looked at Longarm as though he was about to refuse, but after a second glance at the back, he nodded and said, "Very good, señor. If you will follow me."

Longarm rounded the end of the counter and followed the clerk behind the shelves of bakery goods into a large room that was almost as big as the one devoted to customers. This room was filled with the paraphernalia of the baking trade: large tables, racks of trays, long mixing troughs. The air was warmer than that in the other room and the fragrance of baking bread flowed from the arched steel doors of three ovens that broke its back wall. A small glassed office occupied one corner, and in it Longarm saw the back of a man bent over a rolltop desk.

"Is that him?" he asked the clerk.

"Sí, señor. I will tell him—"

"No need for that. You go back to your work. I'll tell him myself."

As Longarm walked across the bakery he took his wallet from his inner coat pocket and held it ready in his hand. He tapped sharply on the glass door and the man at the desk straightened up, looked around, and frowned. Before he could leave his chair Longarm had entered the office.

"You're Mr. Ramon Ortega," he said, hardening his voice

and making his words a statement rather than a question. He gave Ortega no time to reply, and kept him pinned in his chair by pushing the opened wallet so close to Ortega's face that the badge almost touched his nose.

"I am Ramon Ortega," the store owner replied, his voice both puzzled and angry. "But I do not understand—"

Longarm cut him short. "You will, soom as I tell you why I'm here. My name's Long. I'm a deputy United States marshal, and I'm here to arrest you and take you to jail."

"This is foolish!" Ortega protested. "I have broken no law! I am a respectable merchant, and—"

For the second time Longarm cut off Ortega's words. "You'll understand quick enough. Just settle back and listen to what I got to tell you."

Ortega's frown deepened, but he leaned back into his chair. Taking half a step forward, Longarm let the hand holding the badge drop to his side, but did not take his eyes off Ortega's face. Longarm's more than six-foot height towered above the seated merchant and forced him to look up. Gazing down, he suppressed the smile of satisfaction that he felt rising to his lips at the success of the maneuver he had planned. He had placed Ortega in the position of a cowering supplicant gazing upward at a mysterious, menacing giant.

Before Ortega could speak again, Longarm went on, "Don't make no mistakes, Ortega. I'm a federal officer, and my boss is in Washington, D.C., not down at city hall. I ain't one of them San Francisco policemen that's bought and paid for by Abe Ruef. He can't get you out of the fix you're in now."

"I do not understand this!" Ortega repeated, a worried frown creasing his forehead, his lips twitching nervously. "I have broken no law!"

"Aiding and abetting a fugitive from federal law's what I'll be charging you with when I take you to the U.S. Courthouse and have 'em lock you up," Longarm said, pressing his bluff, keeping his voice as hard as the blued steel of his Colt.

"But you have no evidence!" Ortega's worried frown faded for the first time. "Pablo has just returned with the boat! He has had no time to tell . . ." He stopped, his eyes widening as he realized what he had said.

Longarm caught the slip of Ortega's tongue and broke in quickly. "Pablo'll be going to jail with you," he said. "And I guess there'll be more of your men put away, too, soon as we find out how many fugitives from federal law you've helped get away in that boat of yours."

Oretga's resistance crumbled. His shoulders sagged and he dropped his head. "I have been betrayed," he murmured. "My own people have sold me out!"

Longarm saw that it was time for him to pile one last straw on the jerry-built stack he had created to bluff the grocer.

"You likely won't get more'n fifteen or twenty years," he said, his voice still cold and menacing. "That'll depend on how many more federal fugitives you've helped to get away. If I find out you been helping wanted men to escape for a long time, you'll be a real old man before they open the doors to let you out of the Leavenworth federal prison."

Ortega sat silently for a moment, his head bowed despondently. Then he looked up and asked, "Can we not make some kind of arrangement, Marshal Long? Let us say that my men have been using my boat without my knowledge. It could be worth a great deal to you if you testified that I did not know."

"I don't take kindly to being offered bribes, Ortega," Longarm replied, his voice cold.

"Surely there is something . . ."

Ignoring the unhappy man's words, Longarm went on relentlessly, "Of course, if I was able to testify that you helped me by telling me everything you know about this fugitive I'm after, the judge might go a little easier on you."

Ortega grasped at the straw. "What is it you wish to know?"

Even though Longarm could see that his bluff was working, he kept his voice flat and expressionless. He said, "Everything you can tell me about this fellow your men took across the Bay last night. I want to know what he looked like, what he told you, and where you delivered him to. But mind you, I ain't making you no promises. Now, if I catch up with this escaped prisoner I'm looking for, that might be a different kettle of fish."

"I know only a little myself," Ortega said. "The man you are after was a very ugly one, so ugly you would not believe it. He was poorly dressed. He did not ask to be taken to any certain place, but said only that he must find somewhere to hide."

Although he was positive that Ortega's description of the fugitive as being so ugly was all he needed to identify the Stovespit Kid, Longarm went on with his probing. "I don't guess he gave you a name to call him by?"

Shaking his head, Ortega replied, "No. And, for reasons you must surely understand, I did not ask."

"Where'd you deliver him to, then?"

The merchant hesitated. "I cannot tell you that, Marshal Long. I have no right to cause trouble for others."

Longarm made no reply. He reached into the capacious pocket of his coat, pulled out his handcuffs, and dangled them in front of Ortega's face.

Recoiling at the sight of the bright steel cuffs, Ortega no longer hesitated. "Very well," he sighed. "You must know the name anyhow. The man you seek got off my boat at the *rancho* of Joaquin Murietta."

Concealing his surprise, Longarm hardened his voice and said, "Now I know you're lying to me! Joaquin Murietta's been dead twenty years or more! I don't recall who it was killed him, but I heard they cut off his head and put it in a crock of whiskey and showed it off all over the place!"

"That was the first Joaquin." Ortega nodded. "The man I speak of now is his son, who bears the same name. He has a *rancho* on the San Joaquin River, near Stockton."

Longarm had listened to enough lies in the course of his life as a lawman to recognize the truth. His voice still cold, he said, "I sure hope you're telling the truth, Ortega, because you're going to go along with me in that boat to wherever it was your fellows took the man I'm after. And if I find him, I just might forget I ever seen you. Now, get up outa that chair, and let's be moving!"

Chapter 10

Huddled in the stern of the small steam launch, Longarm lighted a fresh cigar and pulled the lapels of his coat together more tightly, trying to shut out the chilling mist that hung low over the surface of the black water. Ortega sat beside him, the collar of his own coat standing up, his head pulled into it, turtle-fashion. Ahead, at the wheel, the man known to Longarm only as Pablo kept his eyes on the winding channel. The other man from Ortega's shop was in the cabin tending to the boiler.

If he had been given a choice, Longarm would have preferred to make the trip in daylight, but he had lost a good part of the afternoon taking care of necessary but time-consuming chores. A visit to the ferry landing to pick up his rifle and saddlebags took an hour, loading the wood chunks that fed the launch's boiler required another hour, and by the time the little vessel steamed north up San Francisco Bay, the last rays of sunset were streaking the Pacific.

Darkness began taking over the sky while the launch steamed up San Pablo Bay and entered Suisun Bay. Midnight found the little craft winding through the delta of the San Joaquin River. After the boat left Suisun Bay, a mist began gathering above the night-black water. It grew thicker while they were passing through the sloughs that connected the scores of streams which formed the river's delta, but as they went deeper inland the mist thinned and lifted a bit until it became a haze that hung only above the waterways.

By the gibbous moonlight, Longarm could see that the land was flat and featureless on each side of the channels. Despite the haze that hung over them, only the water passages reflected the moon's glow. There was little mist above the land, just a few thin wisps that twisted and dissolved as they rose above the surface. The lights of a few widely scattered farmhouses showed as halos when they caught the strands of fog.

"How much farther do we have to go?" Longarm asked.

"A little distance. Not much." Ortega's voice managed to convey a shrug. Then he nodded to a glow that had just become visible on the northern horizon and volunteered, "Those lights you see there are from the town of Stockton. Joaquin's *rancho* is only a short way ahead, another quarter of an hour at the most."

"You've been real helpful so far, Ortega," Longarm said.

With a short, mirthless laugh, the storekeeper replied, "I have had no choice, Marshal."

"Oh, I grant you that. But you oughta come to expect a little upset now and then, when the law catches up with you for helping crooks to get away," Longarm reminded him. "What I'm getting at is, I don't want no trouble outa you or your friend Joaquin Murietta when we get to that ranch of his. That man I'm after ain't worth killing for, but if you or Murietta tries to back me into a corner, I can't make no promises about what might happen to either of you."

"There is no need for you to threaten me," Ortega said. His voice was cold now. "I have no plan to make trouble. I will tell Joaquin that you are interested in only one of his guests, and advise him to surrender the man to you. Will that satisfy you, Marshal Long?"

"As long as I got your word you ain't going to try no tricks on me."

"And do I have yours that if Joaquin surrenders this man you are after, you will take your prisoner and go? That is the bargain we have made, no?"

"That's it," Longarm agreed. "As far as I know, Murietta ain't wanted on any federal charges, and I'll leave the California law to catch up with him sooner or later."

"We are in agreement, then," Ortega said. "Now, if you will look ahead, you can see Joaquin's *rancho*, there on the right-hand bank."

Squinting through the darkness, Longarm could barely

make out the shape of a huddle of buildings in the direction Ortega had indicated. There were three or four structures, but all that he could see was an area of total blackness where their angular lines blocked out the stars. As nearly as he could tell, there were two large buildings and several smaller ones set back from the bank of the slough.

Though no lights showed in any of the structures, their angular lines rising from the dark earth against the lesser darkness of the sky enabled Longarm to guess that the two largest buildings were the main house and barn and the smaller ones were houses for whatever work force Murietta maintained.

"I will tell Pablo to sound our whistle now," Ortega volunteered. "Joaquin will recognize it, and know that we are friends instead of enemies."

"Go ahead." Longarm nodded. "I'd just as soon start off with a clean slate where your outlaw friend's concerned."

"Bocinase, Pablo," Ortega said. *"La seña regular."*

Pablo pulled the lanyard that dangled above the wheel, and three short blasts of the whistle broke the night's stillness. The launch was less than a dozen yards from the narrow wharf that was visible by now, and it lost speed at once when Pablo eased up on its throttle. Longarm saw a rectangle of light appear on the black bulk of one of the buildings. The beam of brightness from the window enabled Longarm to guess that the building from which the light glowed was the main house, and the other sizeable structure was the barn.

By now, Pablo had leaped to the landing and was mooring the launch. Its deck was almost level with the wharf, and Ortega stepped up to the pier at once. Longarm picked up his rifle and followed him. The second of Ortega's men came out of the cabin and joined them.

A man came out of the building where the lighted window still gleamed. He carried a lantern, and as he started toward the landing Longarm glimpsed the glint of its light reflected from the blued steel barrel of the rifle that was tucked in the crook of his elbow.

As the man came closer, Longarm saw that the newcomer wore a short, neatly trimmed beard, had a hawk nose and dark eyes. His head was bare, and his dark hair fell like a black waterfall almost to his shoulders. His clothing was of the type worn by California's original Spanish settlers: a white silk shirt and tight-fitting *vaquero*-style chamois-skin trousers which flared from just below his knees because of a long triangular inset of lace and embroidery.

"*Qué tal, Ramon?*" the newcomer called as soon as he was within easy hailing distance. "*Hay verte ahorita, su lancha era aqui solamente aver.*"

"Do me the favor of speaking English only, Joaquin," Ortega replied. "I have a man with me who does not understand our language."

"Another one so soon, for me to hide?" Murietta asked. His English was virtually without accent. He went on, "I hope he is not as filled with *descortesía* as the other."

"*Cuídarse, amigo!*" Ortega snapped. Then, quickly switching back to English, he went on, "I present to you Deputy United States Marshal Long, Joaquin."

When Ortega spoke the word "deputy," Longarm got the first hint that his guide intended to introduce him to Murietta as a lawman. Before the storekeeper had finished announcing his title and name, Longarm had slipped his derringer from his vest pocket into the palm of his hand. He was ready when Murietta started letting his rifle slide from the crook of his elbow.

Before Murietta could grasp the wrist of his rifle's stock and get his finger on the trigger, Longarm sent a slug from the derringer into the boards of the wharf between the outlaw's feet, then raised the muzzle of the deadly little weapon. Murietta's jaw dropped as he stared into the derringer's twin barrels.

"Don't try to lift that rifle, Murietta!" Longarm said. His tone was conversational, but his voice was steel-hard, and the unwavering muzzle of the derringer added a silent threat.

Instead of closing his hand over the wrist of the rifle's stock as he had planned, Murietta let the rifle slide through his fingers. It clattered to the boards of the wharf.

Longarm went on. "I ain't got any bad feeling toward you yet, and I ain't here to make you any trouble. You got a man I'm after in your place here. He's the one Ortega sent you."

91

"I admit nothing!" Murietta snapped.

"You don't have to admit nothing," Longarm retorted. "I know he's here, and he's the only reason I come visiting you. I don't give two hoots in hell if you're hiding men on the run in every room of your house. All I'm interested in is the one I want."

While he was speaking, Longarm shifted the derringer to his left hand and casually raised the muzzle of the Winchester until it was within inches of Murietta's waist.

Ortega said hastily, "Do what Marshal Long asks, Joaquin! He will take his prisoner and leave at once, and you will suffer no harm."

"My good name will be lost if I surrender a man who has sought shelter with me!" the outlaw rasped through his clenched teeth. "I cannot do this, Ramon!"

"I got six good reasons in this rifle to make you change your mind, Murietta," Longarm said quietly. His voice was as cold as the black water that lapped against the dock on which they stood. "And there's five more just as good in my Colt."

Ortega added his voice to the argument. "Be reasonable, Joaquin! Marshal Long will leave at once to take this man far from here! No one will know what you have done!"

"I will know!" Murietta retorted. Then, in his anger and agitation, he dropped into Spanish and added, *"Es un cosa de pundonor, Ramon!"*

Though Longarm's understanding of Spanish was limited, he understood Murietta's reference to his honor. He said, "Things like pride and honor don't cut no ice with me. Now, there's just two things you can do. You can try to pick up that rifle of yours and get a bullet through you. Or you can walk back with me to your house and hand over that man I'm after. Which one is it going to be?"

Murietta stood silently for a moment, his face inscrutable. At last he shrugged and said, "I cannot argue with your reasons, señor. If you wish to follow me to the house, I will surrender the man you want."

"That's right sensible of you," Longarm said. Turning to Ortega, he added, "You and your men better go first. I don't

92

want you between me and Murietta. Just walk slow and easy, and nobody needs to get hurt."

Ortega nodded to his men and they started toward the house. Murietta turned to follow them, still carrying the lantern, and Longarm joined the little procession as soon as he had hunkered down long enough to pick up the rifle Murietta had let fall. They had covered less than half the distance to the house when the faint light that had been shining from the upper window was suddenly extinguished. Glass tinkled from one of the dark windows of the lower floor. A rifle barked, its muzzle-flash spurted red in the darkness, and one of Ortega's men stumbled and went down.

A streak of light cut through the darkness as Murietta flung the lantern in a high arc that sent it sailing into the slough. It landed with a splash, and the darkness that blotted out the path was broken only by the faint starshine.

Longarm brought up his Winchester, but he was blinded in the sudden darkness. Blinking fast as he tried to regain his night vision, he started toward the house, letting off a blind snapshot in the general direction of the fading sounds made by the footfalls of men running toward the house. The footsteps did not change rhythm.

From the house another shot cut the night, and Longarm heard the slug whistle above his head. Realizing that he must be silhouetted against the sky, he dived forward and fell into a tangle of arms and legs.

"*Se muerte Pablo!*" Ortega said. "*Era un buen—*"

"Shut up!" Longarm snapped. He was getting back to his feet as he spoke. "Them fellows in the house ain't going to quit shooting. We got to get away from here fast!"

"But Joaquin would not shoot me!" Ortega protested.

"They can't tell which one of us is which! Both of us is going to wind up dead as your man is if we don't get outa here!"

Underlining Longarm's words, two shots barked from the house and bullets whistled past them, but both were high.

Longarm was on his feet by now. He left the two rifles on the ground while he groped for the collar of Ortega's coat and dragged the storekeeper unceremoniously to his feet.

"You can't help Pablo," Longarm said harshly. "Come on! If we head for that barn, we both got a chance to stay alive!"

Another shot rang out from the house and kicked up dirt in front of Pablo's corpse. It was more convincing than Longarm's words had been. Ortega started toward the barn at a run. Longarm scooped up both rifles and ran beside him.

Darkness covered their sudden move. Before they had reached the barn, two more widely spaced shots from the house sent lead shrilling above the dead man's body and into the water of the slough. During the interval between the shots, Longarm and Ortega were in the relative safety of the cavernous structure. Though the gloom within the barn was a bit deeper than that outside, Longarm's eyes had adjusted to the darkness once more, and he could see that the stalls along each side of the barn's walls all held horses.

"Looks to me like your friend Murietta takes real good care of his stock," he commented. "Keeps his horses in here instead of in a corral."

"These are his special horses," Ortega said. "The ones he uses in working his *rancho* are in corrals beyond this barn."

"What do you mean, special horses?"

"They are called palominos. Always when I visit Joaquin he insists that I come here with him to look at his highly bred horses, but I have small interest in such things. I accompany him only to please him."

"You mean these horses is all thoroughbreds?"

"But of course. And they are all handsome. It is Joaquin's great interest to have such fine horseflesh at his command."

Longarm had started walking along the stalls, counting the horses, before Ortega had finished. He said thoughtfully, "I imagine these nags are worth a good bit of money. And there's sixteen of 'em, so if your friend Murietta stood to lose a few, it'd sorta set him back a few steps."

"He would be desolated at the thought of losing even one."

"Maybe we ain't in such bad shape after all," Longarm went on. "I got to move fast, though. I figure we only got a few minutes before Murietta gets his men after us. You think he'd listen to you if you yelled at him and said you wanted to talk?"

"But of course he would!"

Longarm had been squinting upward while they talked, trying to pierce the darkness with his eyes. He asked Ortega, "I guess you'd remember the layout of this barn, since you been here before. Ain't there a hayloft running along the sides over these horse stalls?"

"Yes, it is a special kind of hay, very expensive."

Longarm felt his way along the stalls until he found the ladder that led up to the loft. He mounted only high enough to enable him to pull a sizeable bunch of hay from the loft to the floor. Dropping back down the ladder, he bundled a small handful of hay together, closed his eyes to slits, and touched a match to the hay. It flared up at once, revealing the double line of stalls, each holding a golden horse with a white mane. Longarm lifted his improvised torch while he squinted along the stalls. A few of the horses stamped and tossed their heads at the sudden light. Then his eyes reached the end of the row and he saw that, as he'd surmised, the barn had double doors at both ends. He turned back to Ortega.

"Now, here's what I want you to do," he said. "Take this bunch of hay over to the door so's Murietta can see it's you. Tell him he's got three minutes to bring the Stovespit Kid out here. If he don't, I'll start shooting his horses."

"But, Marshal Long—" Oretga began.

"Shut up and do what I told you to! Murietta's already killed one of your men, and I don't reckon he'd think twice about shooting you."

"No! Joaquin is my friend!"

"You might've thought he was before you brought me here," Longarm said, his voice cold. "I'll bet dollars to doughnuts he don't call you his friend any longer. Now, get over to the door and start calling him!"

Reluctance showing in his every move, Ortega took the wisp of burning hay and walked to the open door of the barn. Holding the makeshift torch above his head, he called, "Joaquin! I must talk with you!"

After a moment of silence, Murietta's voice replied, "We have nothing to talk about, Ramon!"

Longarm moved quickly to the door of the barn, keeping well behind its half-opened doors. "You better listen to Ortega!" he shouted. "All he wants to ask you is would you like to have these palomino horses of yours shot!"

"You would not do such a thing!" Murietta called back.

Unexpectedly, Ortega spoke before Longarm could reply. "Do not deceive yourself, Joaquin! Marshal Long would do just as he has told you!"

"Es barbaridad!" Murietta yelled, his voice rising almost to a falsetto as in his excitement he dropped into his mother language. *"Si hace este, matarles lo mismo!"*

Longarm understood enough Spanish to understand the threat, and crowded all the authority he could muster into his voice as he replied, "You'll do what I tell you to!" As he spoke, he took a match from his vest pocket, extended his hand beyond the door jamb, and flicked it into flame with his thumbnail. "Or I'll toss this match into your hayloft. You ever hear a horse scream when it was caught in a stable on fire, Murietta?"

For a long moment, Murietta did not reply. When he did, his voice was less strident, almost subdued. "What do you want from me, Marshal Long?" he asked.

"I want the man Ortega sent you from San Francisco yesterday," Longarm replied. The match he held was beginning to burn low and he let it fall, lighting another one to take its place. "I don't know what name he's travelling under, but I call him the Stovespit Kid."

Murietta snorted inelegantly. "A hundred like him are not worth one of my palominos! He is yours."

"Then prod him out here where I can see him," Longarm said. "As soon as I put my handcuffs on him, I'll take him and leave."

"You say you will leave with him, but how do I know I can trust you?" Murietta called.

"You don't, any more'n I know I can trust you," Longarm called back. "But I got a hunch we can both trust your friend Ortega. Am I right?"

For a moment Murietta did not answer. Then he said, "Ramon has been my friend for many years, and in spite of my anger I will trust him, if you do. What is your plan?"

"My saddlebags are on Ortega's boat. They got my handcuffs in 'em, and that Stovespit Kid is so slippery I ain't taking him anyplace until he's got the cuffs on. While Ortega goes down to get the boat fired up and ready to move, you fetch the Stovespit Kid outside, where I can get a good look at him."

"And if I do this, you will agree not to disturb my palominos?" Murietta asked.

"Soon as Ortega gets my handcuffs back here and puts 'em on the Kid, I'll take him and go. The boat'll be ready to move by then," Longarm replied.

Again Murietta was silent for a moment. Then he said, "I must talk to Ramon first."

"He's standing right here by me. Go on and have your say," Longarm invited the outlaw.

"Ramon," Murietta called, "if you will help me save my horses, I will forget this trouble you have brought me. Will you do as the marshal says?"

"You know that I will, Joaquin," Ortega answered quickly. "I do not wish to see your blood or his spilled because of a stupid mistake I have made."

"Go, then!" Murietta said. "I will get the man he wants and bring him here."

Murietta disappeared into the house, and Ortega started toward the landing. Longarm stood in the door of the barn, gazing thoughtfully into the darkness.

Chapter 11

As soon as Ortega was lost in the night's gloom, Longarm hurried back into the barn. He struck another match and looked around quickly. As he had anticipated, there were saddles on a rack just inside the door and bridles hanging on nails driven into the wooden wall above them. He pulled down two of the bridles and returned hurriedly to the back of the barn.

Working as fast as he could in the darkness, Longarm put the bridles on the palominos in the last two stalls and led them out to the center of the barn. The big double door in the back was secured by a heavy wooden crossbar. He removed the bar and cast it aside, opened the doors just wide enough to let a horse pass through, then led the pair he had bridled to the opening and tethered them to the L-shaped boards that had supported the crossbar.

Knowing that his time must be running out, Longarm started back to the door facing the house. As he moved he zigzagged from side to side, tripping the latches that secured the gates of the horse stalls. Stretching his long legs to the utmost, he reached the front of the barn just in time to scoop up his rifle before the door of the big house opened and Murietta came out, pushing the Stovespit Kid ahead of him.

While in the house, Murietta had lighted another lantern, and was holding it high in his left hand. His revolver was in his right hand, its muzzle prodding the Stovespit Kid in the ribs. The Kid's ugly face was twisted in anger, his thick lips flapping.

"Damn it, Murietta, I paid you lots of money for a safe hidey-hole! You ain't got no right to roust me around this way!" the Stovespit Kid was saying.

"Cállate, cabrón!" Murietta snapped.

Ortega came into the circle of light cast by the lantern. He carried Longarm's saddlebags in one hand.

"Well, damn you, too!" the Kid exploded when he saw the grocer. "I guess both of you sons of bitches was in cahoots to sell me out!"

"He dijo cállate!" Murietta growled.

He brought the revolver up and slapped the Kid on the side of the head with its barrel. The Kid let out a yowl of pain, and Murietta hit him for a second time. The Kid's head dropped, and he stood swaying, on the verge of being knocked out.

"That's enough, Murietta!" Longarm called. "Ortega, get the handcuffs out of my saddlebags and put 'em on the Stovespit Kid. And don't try no tricks on me! I'll be keeping an eye on you!"

"No tricks, señor," Ortega promised.

He took the cuffs out of Longarm's saddlebags and moved to the Stovespit Kid, who was still so close to being unconscious that he made no effort to struggle when the steel manacles closed around his wrists.

"Here is your prisoner, Marshal Long," Murietta said when Ortega finished cuffing the Kid and stepped aside. "Come and get him. I will be glad to see the last of both of you."

"Not so fast!" Longarm replied. "I ain't fool enough to trust you in back of me, Murietta. You and Ortega start walking down to the landing. Now that I've got the Kid back, I don't aim to let him get outa my sight."

For a moment, Murietta hesitated, but when Ortega obeyed Longarm's command and turned to go back down the path to the landing, Murietta shrugged and followed him. Longarm waited for a moment to let them gain a bit of distance, then stepped up to the Stovespit Kid.

"Come on," he commanded. "Me and you got some travelling to do. If you're half-smart, you'll do what I say. I'd rather let a judge and jury handle you, but unless you hop when I say jump, you might not ever get into court."

"You don't scare me a damn bit, Long!" the Kid sneered. "I was smart enough to give you the slip in Oakland, so I guess I can find a way to do it again."

"We ain't got time to stand here and jaw now," Longarm told him. "Come on! And I'll warn you again, don't try none of your damn tricks on me."

Grasping his rifle firmly in one hand, Longarm closed his free hand on the chain that connected the Kid's wrist shackles and led him toward the barn.

"Hey!" the Kid protested. "The landing's down in the other direction! Where the hell are you taking me?"

"You'll find out fast!" Longarm snapped, giving the chain a sudden jerk that caused the Kid to stumble and almost fall. "Now walk, or I'll drag you along with me."

Longarm jerked the chain again, and the Kid took a step forward to save himself from falling on his face. Once they had started, Longarm showed his prisoner no mercy. The cuffs on the Kid's wrists bit into the flesh as he stumbled with Longarm to the barn. Inside, his eyes straining through the gloom, Longarm reversed the zigzag path he had followed earlier as he moved from stall to stall, rousting out the palominos and driving them toward the open doors at the back.

Neighing in protest, rearing and jostling, the horses were forced down the center of the barn and out the open doors. When only the two animals which Longarm had fitted with bridles were left, Longarm took a match from his vest pocket, scraped his thumbnail over its head, and tossed the burning match into the small pile of hay he had dragged from the loft.

Once ignited, the hay burst into flames quickly. The few strands that straggled down the ladder caught and carried the blaze into the loft, setting off the main supply. Within a few seconds the hayloft turned into a blazing inferno. Longarm did not need to drag his prisoner down the center of the barn to the two tethered horses. The Stovespit Kid went willingly, watching the flames in the hayloft racing to engulf the entire barn.

"Swing onto one of 'em!" Longarm told the Kid when they got to the two tethered palominos. He released his grip on the handcuff chain and grabbed the reins of the palomino that his prisoner mounted, then leaped to the back of the second horse. "Now, hang on, you ugly son of a bitch! We got some riding to do before Murietta sees that fire and comes running back!"

Digging his heels into the palomino's flanks, Longarm

100

yanked the reins of the horse the Kid had mounted, and the spooked animals dashed into the open. Flames had already eaten through the shingled roof in several places now, outlining the main house in sharp relief and lighting up the flat land for a hundred yards in all directions. As Longarm glanced back, letting the palomino pick its own way, he got a glimpse of Joaquin Murietta and Ortega running from the landing toward the burning barn.

By this time the horses he had freed from their stalls were in motion, beginning to scatter in their panic as they ran from the flames. Their excited neighing and whinnying cut through the still night air above the crackling of the flames, their golden bodies etched against the blackness beyond the constantly expanding circle of light.

Suddenly the quiet was broken by a series of explosions as the heat of the fire got to the ammunition in the magazine of the rifle Longarm had taken from Murietta and had left behind in the burning barn. The loud popping of the shells as they exploded broke the quiet night and sent a gout of flame high into the sky, which was already illuminated by the blaze. Longarm could see the figures of Murietta and Ortega silhouetted against the glare as they circled around the burning barn, their arms waving in wild gesticulations.

"I guess I ain't been giving you enough credit, Marshal," the Stovespit Kid commented grudgingly as Longarm reined in and turned to look back. "You put on a real good show."

"I don't need no jaw-flap outa you," Longarm snapped. "But maybe you'll get the idea that it won't do you a bit of good to try pulling your tricks on me while we're on our way back to Denver."

"Oh, I got a few tricks left up my sleeve," the Kid boasted. "You ain't seen all of 'em yet. Don't lay too much store on getting me back. Colorado's a hell of a long ways from California."

"Too long to suit me, because I'm already tired of looking at you and listening to your jaws wag. You just shut up and ride. We're still too close to Murietta's place for me to feel real comfortable, too."

"You don't have to worry about him," the Kid said. "If it

makes you feel any better, Joaquin sent all his hands to town to buy grub and some other stuff. You've handed him a fistful of trouble. He won't be likely to take after us."

"Damned if you don't sound almost human sometimes," Longarm said with a frown. "Not that I'll be fooled by it. Now, let's get moving again. From what I recall about this part of the country, we ain't too far from Stockton, and I'll rest a lot easier when I get you in a set of leg irons and on the train."

Finding a road that would take him and the Stovespit Kid to Stockton took much more time than Longarm had anticipated. The maze of branches and sloughs that formed the crazy-quilt pattern of the San Joaquin River's delta turned what would normally have been half a day's ride into a nightmare of wandering and backtracking. There were few bridges across the slough and creeks. Time after time, Longarm and his prisoner were forced to backtrack after taking what looked to be a well-travelled path, only to wind up at a farmhouse or on the banks of a wide stream of brown, sluggishly flowing water.

Late in the morning, at the third farmhouse where they had stopped to get directions, Longarm finally decided to cut his losses.

"Look here," he said to the farmer after listening to a five-minute explanation of which unmarked turns to take and which paths led where, "I'll make you a proposition. If you'll hitch up your wagon and carry me and my prisoner into Stockton, I'll give you a federal voucher for ten dollars."

"Whatever a federal voucher is, I ain't needed one yet, and it don't seem likely I will, Marshal," the man said. "Now, if you was to offer me cash, I might think on the notion."

"I'm running short of cash," Longarm explained. "The only place I can draw some more is from a federal marshal's office, and the closest one is either in San Francisco or Sacramento. I just plain don't have time to waste traipsing over half of California. But you can take this voucher into any bank and get cash for it. It's just like you'd be handing 'em a check."

"Don't trust banks," the farmer said, shaking his head. "Had to sell a fine farm I owned back in Ioway when a bank went bust. Ain't sure I trust the federal government ten dollars' worth, either. If it was cash in advance, now—"

"Try offering him fifteen, Long," the Stovespit Kid broke in. "Providing he'll dish us up some breakfast before we start. My belly thinks my throat's been cut."

"You keep your mouth outa this!" Longarm snapped. "I don't need you to tell me what to do."

"Ten or fifteen, it wouldn't make no difference," the farmer said. "I got to seed my south field before the day's out. If I put off doing my work, it's likely to start raining again, and I'll get so far behind I can't catch up."

Longarm had a sudden inspiration. "I seen you looking real close at these horses we're riding," he said. "I guess you know what kind they are?"

"Why, sure," the man nodded. "Palominos. There's a Mexican fellow over on the north slough that's got a bunch of 'em. Costly critters, I've heard, and they're real pretty, but they're riding horses. They ain't no good for farm work."

"I wasn't figuring to sell 'em," Longarm said. "This man you mentioned over on the north slough, do you know him?"

"Nope." The farmer shook his head. "Heard he's some kinda outlaw, though."

"His name's Murietta," Longarm said. "I had to make a sorta unofficial requisition to use these horses on government business. How much do you figure he'd pay to get 'em back?"

"Hard to say. Maybe as much as ten dollars apiece, I'd guess."

"More likely twenty or thirty apiece," Longarm said. "And he's got the money in ready cash, too."

"Sounds like you're trying to make another kind of deal with me now, Marshal." The farmer frowned. "If I see what you're getting at, you want me to haul you and your prisoner to Stockton in my wagon, and you'll give me a paper that you say's worth ten dollars. Then you'll throw in the horses for me to take back to this Murietta fellow and claim a reward?"

"That's about the size of it," Longarm said. "I got to get this prisoner back to Denver as fast as I can, and I can't lose a day or two floundering around in these damned sloughs."

"Well, now, if you'd told me that in the first place, I

might've hauled you there free," the farmer said slowly. "But if you'll stand by that last deal you offered, I guess I'll go on and accommodate you. Ride around to the barn and I'll hitch up the wagon."

Dusk was creeping across the sky when the farmer's wagon creaked into Stockton. Longarm was very tired after two almost sleepless nights in a row, and he had taken no chances of allowing the Stovespit Kid to escape. Before they had started the trip, he had unlocked the manacle on the Kid's right wrist and closed it around his own left wrist. The Stovespit Kid had stretched out in the wagon bed and gone to sleep. Longarm had tried to sleep also, but each time the Kid moved his right arm, Longarm's left arm got a sudden jerk. As a result, he'd been able to manage only a few minutes of fitful dozing during the slow, jolting wagon ride.

When the farmer pulled up his horse in front of the Stockton police station, Longarm was glad to get out, even though he did not unlock the cuffs to make alighting easier. He took his wallet from the inside breast pocket of his coat and took out one of his voucher forms.

"I'll have to go inside and get a pencil to fill this out with," he said. "In case you're afraid I won't come back, I'll leave my saddlebags and rifle with you."

Inside the building, Longarm stopped at the duty sergeant's desk and took out his wallet. Flipping it open to show his badge, he said, "Custis Long, deputy U.S. marshal, Sergeant. I sure hope you got a cell where I can park this prisoner of mine till the next through train to the east comes through here."

"Always glad to oblige a fellow officer, Marshall Long," the sergeant replied, extending his hand over the desk for Longarm to shake. "We've got plenty of room for your man. Just take the cuffs off him and we'll tuck him away."

"Now, I better tell you, this fellow's slick," Longarm went on as he inserted the key in the handcuff shackle on his wrist. He unlocked the steel semicircle and and snapped it on the Kid's left wrist. "You'll book him in under the name of

Chauncey Mahoney, but he's better known as the Stovespit Kid."

"Is he the one that got out of the Oakland jail a few days ago?" the sergeant asked.

"That's him. He don't look like much, but he's a slick one."

"So I've heard," the sergeant nodded. "I hear he got his nickname because he's like a blob you'd spit on a hot stove— just a little sizzle and he disappears."

"That's what I been told, too," Longarm said. "Now, I need to use your pen to—" He broke off and turned to look at the Kid. Where his prisoner had been standing a few seconds earlier there was only empty space. He said over his shoulder as he started for the station door, "If you got a whistle handy, you better blow it! The son of a bitch has done it again!"

Springing from his chair, the police sergeant stepped to the wall and jerked a lever. Bells began clanging throughout the building, and Longarm heard excited voices approaching down the hall as he dashed for the front door. There was no one on the sidewalk outside the police station, and no one visible in the street except the farmer sitting on the seat of his wagon.

"Did you see my prisoner come out?" Longarm asked.

"I ain't seen a soul since you and him went inside," the man replied. "You mean he's got away?"

"It sure looks like it, but he can't be far off," Longarm replied. "He ain't had time—" Longarm stopped short and drew his Colt in a single flashing sweep of his arm. Hunkering down beside the wagon, he levelled the pistol at the Stovespit Kid, who was lying stretched out in the semi-darkness underneath the wagon bed.

"All right, Kid," Longarm said. "You better come out now. I ain't in a very good humor, and my arm's tired from you pulling on it all day. My finger just might pull the trigger accidental-like, if you take a notion to act up."

With a deep sigh, the Kid rolled from beneath the wagon and got to his feet. "I wasn't sure I could make it," he said cheerfully. "You was just too close, and it's nowhere near dark enough, but I figured I had to try, anyhow."

"You try again and you might not get off so easy," Long-arm warned him. "I got a hunch I'd save myself a lot of trouble if I could just ship you back to Denver in a casket in the baggage car." Grabbing the Kid's arm, he went on, "Now, let's get back inside. I aim to see you locked up myself, and you won't get outa my sight until I turn you over to the jailer in Denver!"

Chapter 12

"Well, I sure did enjoy my breakfast," Longarm told the police sergeant as he pushed away his plate and took out a cigar. "This is the first time I ever put away a jail meal that tasted like it was meant to be served up to people."

"It's easier for us to serve decent food here than it is in a lot of jails," the sergeant said. "The farmers in the valley bring their truck here because they can ship it to San Francisco cheaper on boats than on the train, and there's plenty of cattle on the hoof close by."

"It was right tasty," Longarm said, exhaling a cloud of blue smoke before picking up his coffee cup for a final swallow. "I guess I better get back in the cell with my prisoner now," Longarm went on. "You said I got almost two hours before train time, didn't you?"

"About that. Stockton's not on the main line, you know. You'll have to make connections with the eastbound Limited in Sacramento. Now, if there's anything more we can do . . ."

As the sergeant let his question trail off, Longarm said, "You know, I just happened to think about it, but there just might be. That Stovespit Kid is about the slipperiest man I ever run into. On the way back I'll have to change trains with him in Sacramento and again in Cheyenne, and I'd feel better if he was wearing leg irons and handcuffs both."

"I noticed he was still in handcuffs when I came to call you to breakfast," the sergeant said.

"And he might not've been there at all if I'd took the cuffs off him. I tell you, he's a real getaway artist. That's why I got to wondering if you could make me the loan of a set of leg irons for the trip back."

"I'm sure we can," the sergeant said, "but they'd be the old-style ones, connected with a chain instead of a pair of swivel bars. We changed to the new kind a little while back, but we kept the old ones just in case."

"That don't matter to me one bit. And I'll send yours back just as soon as I got my man safe behind bars in Denver."

"All I've got to do is dig a pair out of the supply room. It won't take a minute."

True to his word, the sergeant was back within a very few minutes. He carried a set of leg irons, oversized shackles with individual padlocks to go around each ankle, connected by a three-foot length of stout chain. Handing them to Longarm, he said, "I've only got one key. It opens both padlocks, and I don't suppose you'll be needing a spare."

"It ain't likely I would," Longarm answered. "I'll tuck this one away where it'll be safe, and feel my wallet every now and then to make sure the Kid ain't managed to steal it."

"You mean he's a pickpocket, too?"

"As far as I know, he ain't," Longarm said. He smiled and added, "But it wouldn't surprise me if he was. If you don't mind letting me use your spare key to open his cell, I'll just go put these irons on him now. Maybe he'll get a little bit used to them by the time I take him to the train."

Only the Stovespit Kid and three prisoners who were still sleeping off their liquor in the drunk tank occupied the city jail when Longarm opened its heavy door. The jail was typical of many others Longarm had seen in small cities during his years as a lawman. Narrow, barred windows set high in the outer wall provided light. It had four cells which each held two narrow bunks and a drunk tank that was twice the size of the cells and contained four bunks. Vertical iron bars separated the cells.

In the cell next to the drunk tank the Stovespit Kid was sitting on a bunk. The mattress was only a little thicker than a man's flattened hand and the bunk had no pillows. In the corner of the cell there was a covered slop jar. When the Stovespit Kid saw the leg irons Longarm was carrying a frown formed on his face, making it look more lopsided than usual.

"Hold on there!" he protested. "If you think I'm going to

108

wear them damn irons all the way back to Denver, you got another think coming! I'll see hell freeze up before I put them on!"

"You ain't got nothing at all to say about whether you put 'em on or not," Longarm reminded him. "And if you take a good close look at hell, you're likely to find it's snowing down there about now. Now, I'll tell you something else. You'll wear these irons day and night till we get to Denver, even if they do happen to give you bad dreams."

"Now, that just ain't fair!" the Kid went on. "How in hell do you figure I can get on or off of a train? If it was a slow freight, maybe, but not a fast train like the Limited!"

"I got a hunch that if you can scheme up a way to do it, you'll make a stab at jumping off the train, regardless," Longarm said unsympathetically. "Or you would, if your legs was free. Now, sit down on your bunk while I harness you up."

"Don't put too much store in that contraption, Long," the Kid cautioned Longarm as he sat down and stretched out his legs. "I'll find a way to beat it."

"And I'll find a way to see you don't," Longarm said. He snapped the padlock through the hasp of one of the shackles as he was talking, and lifted the chain to let it straighten out before attaching the shackle to the Kid's other ankle. "Now, we still got a little time before we leave for the depot, so you better practice walking in them things."

"Maybe I'll decide I don't want to walk if I've got to haul a bunch of iron along with every step I take," the Kid told him. "What'd you do if I did that, Mr. United States Marshal?"

Longarm was lighting a cheroot and made no reply until he had it drawing to his satisfaction. When he spoke, his voice was flat, and held no emotion at all.

"Why, I'd likely just grab that chain and drag you," he said. "Pretty soon you'd get tired of bouncing along and get up and walk like a human being. Not that you are one."

For a moment the Stovespit Kid stared at Longarm, his thick eyebrows upraised and bristling. Then he said, "By God, I think that's what you'd really do!"

"Don't make no mistake about it," Longarm warned him. "All the bumps you'd get on your head wouldn't hurt me one

109

damned bit. You think on it a while. I'll be back to get you when it's time to go to the depot."

Satisfied that the combination of prison bars and leg irons would keep the Stovespit Kid from escaping during the next two hours, Longarm put his time to good use. The jail was only a short distance from Stockton's business section. He walked along the store-lined streets until he found a saloon that had a stock of Tom Moore Maryland rye, had a belated eye-opener, and bought a bottle to carry on the train. Then he stopped in the tobacco shop next door to the saloon and replenished his stock of cigars. Carrying his purchases, he returned to the jail and tucked them into his saddlebags.

"I guess it's close enough to train time for me to be heading for the depot with my prisoner," he told the desk sergeant. "If you'll pass me your blotter, I'll sign him out, and then you'll be rid of him."

"Do you want me to send the turnkey for him?" the sergeant asked. "It'll save you walking back to the jail, and while you're waiting you can be signing these forms I've got to send to the federal marshal's office in San Francisco so the city can get paid for feeding your man and holding him overnight."

"Sure," Longarm nodded. "Just pass 'em over, and I'll sign 'em. You folks have been real nice, and I wouldn't want you to be short-changed."

As familiar as he was with federal paperwork, Longarm made a quick job of scrawling his signature on the forms. He was just handing them back to the sergeant when the turnkey ran in. His eyes were wide with shocked surprise and a deep frown corrugated his forehead.

"Sergeant!" he stammered. "You'd better ring the alarm bell quick! That federal prisoner's got away! His cell's empty!"

"Are you sure?" the sergeant asked, stepping to the wall behind his desk and pumping a lever that started a clamor of distant bells echoing in the building.

For a moment, Longarm had the feeling that he was back in Oakland, repeating his experience of a few days past. Before the turnkey could say anything more, Longarm volunteered, "He was there just before I went out, and that wasn't more'n fifteen or twenty minutes ago."

"Well, he's sure not in his cell now, Marshal," the turnkey said positively. "You can go look for yourself if you want to, but you won't find him there."

Turning to the sergeant, Longarm said, "The Stovespit Kid ain't going to get very far with them leg irons I put on him. But I don't guess you heard that he pulled a trick just like this when he got outa the Oakland holdover a few days back. Now, I imagine that bell you rung is a sorta general alarm?"

"That's right," the sergeant nodded. "This building only has three outside doors, and by this time there'll be men covering all of them."

"Now, in Oakland, the Kid hid out in a closet or maybe a clothes locker until things quieted down," Longarm said with a thoughtful frown. "Nobody missed him for quite a while, and by the time they started looking for him he'd put on a uniform that belonged to one of the officers and walked out as cool as you please. I'd sorta guess he's trying to do the same thing here."

"We'll search the building, don't worry about that," the sergeant promised. "And if you'd like to help, you're sure welcome to. You know more about this Stovespit Kid than we do."

"Maybe so, but your men would know more about this building than me," Longarm replied. I'll just stay outa their way."

"Suit yourself," the sergeant said. "Chances are that we'll dig him out of wherever he's found cover. In Stockton there aren't too many places for a man wearing leg irons to hide."

"Come to think of it, I didn't hear your turnkey say anything about them leg irons I put on the Kid," Longarm said. "If it's all the same to you, and you'll make me a loan of that spare key again, I'll go take a look at the cell you put the Kid in. Maybe I'd see something there that your men would miss."

"I'll call you when we turn him up," the sergeant told him.

Longarm made his way to the cellblock. The turnkey's desk just outside the jail door was unoccupied and he guessed that the man was joining the search being made of the building. When he passed the desk and went into the right-angle corridor that led to the cellblock, he saw the door leading into it was ajar, and realized that in his excitement the turnkey had failed to close it when he dashed out of the block to report his missing prisoner.

Entering the cellblock, Longarm glanced at the three men in the drunk tank. Each of them was still fast asleep, one of them face up, another face down, the third on his side. As nearly as Longarm recalled, their positions were unchanged from the time of his first visit. The door of the cell was closed, and he gave the sleepers no more than the passing survey needed to assure him that the occupants were in no condition to have helped the Kid in his latest disappearance.

He moved on to the cell the Stovespit Kid had occupied. It too was vacant, the door closed and locked. Using the key he'd gotten from the sergeant, Longarm went in and stood in the center of the barred cubicle while he studied the bare area inch by inch.

What you're looking at just downright ain't possible, old son, he told himself silently. *There ain't one thing more or less in this damned cell than there was an hour ago, except that the Stovespit Kid's gone. The mattresses on them bunks ain't thick enough for him to be hiding in one of 'em, and the chamber pot ain't big enough. So you got to be looking at something and not seeing it. There ain't no way in the world for the Stovespit Kid to be hiding in here, and there ain't no way he could've got out. So there ain't no two ways about it, he's got to be here, even if you can't see him.*

A sudden snort of rasping snores followed by a sneeze drew Longarm's attention to the drunk tank. He peered through the bars between the two cells, but could see no change in the positions of the sleeping trio. He was about to return his attention to the cell in which he was standing when a thought struck him.

Wait a minute, old son, he told himself. *There ain't a man living that can snort out that much of a sneeze without moving around a little bit. And none of them three fellows in that drunk-tank cell has moved a muscle. Maybe it'd be a good idea for you to take a closer look in there.*

112

Longarm moved up to the bars which separated the drunk tank from the cell in which he stood and began examining the tank and its occupants with an inch-by-inch scrutiny.

Unlike the narrow rectangular cell in which Longarm stood, the drunk tank was square, occupying a corner of the jail area. Two of its four bunks were on the building's outside wall. The others were on the wall of a partition that extended into the building. Two of the drunks were in bunks fixed to the outer wall; the third bunk was at right angles to them.

Longarm fixed his attention first on the occupants of the two bunks closest to him. They lay supine; the slight rise and fall of their chests as they breathed was the only movement he saw in their recumbent forms. As he shifted his eyes to the third drunk, Longarm saw the man's body twitch. He said nothing, but kept watching. Almost imperceptibly, the drunk twitched again.

Smiling inwardly, Longarm moved silently. He left the cell and took the two steps needed to reach the drunk tank. The key that unlocked the cell which had been occupied by the Stovespit Kid also opened the drunk-tank door.

Drawing his Colt as he moved, Longarm went to the bunk on the partition wall. Now his eyes were above the narrow bunk and what he saw when he looked down transformed his inner smile into an open grin. Unlike the other drunk-tank occupants, who were sprawled fully dressed and uncovered, this man had a blanket drawn up to his chin. Holding the Colt ready, Longarm leaned forward and stripped away the blanket.

"All right, Kid," he said casually. "You can get up now. It's time to start back to Denver."

"God damn you for being such a smart son of a bitch, Long!" the Stovespit Kid grated as he stared into the Colt's muzzle. "I guess I didn't give you enough credit!"

"I guess you didn't," Longarm agreed. "Your trick was slick enough, but that sneeze give you away. Not that I was going to stop till I found you. Sneeze or no sneeze, I'd've tumbled to your trick."

"All I needed was another two or three minutes and I'd've been clear away!" the Kid complained as he lifted himself from behind the sleeping drunk. The leg irons hampered his movements, but Longarm made no effort to help him as he maneuvered himself to the floor.

"Get back to your own cell," Longarm commanded. Sullenly silent, the Kid shuffled with short, clumsy steps out of the drunk tank, and entered the cell in which he had been confined. "You just sit down and wait a minute," Longarm went on. "I got to go to the door and tell the officers you're still here. Then you and me have got a little bit of unfinished business to settle that I ain't had time to take care of until now."

Longarm's shout down the corridor was enough to inform the police searchers that the Stovespit Kid's effort to escape had been thwarted. He returned to the cell and stood in the door for a moment, his eyes as cold as icicles in January, as he stared at his prisoner.

"Well, what the hell are you waiting for?" the Kid asked after he had endured Longarm's silent scrutiny for a minute or so. "If you've got some unfinished business, why don't you get on with it and get out? I don't mind telling you, Long, I'm tired of looking at you!"

"You ain't no right pretty sight yourself," Longarm said. "And I don't guess you'll look any better when you stand up and get all your clothes stripped off."

"Wait a minute now!" the Kid protested. "You've got no right to—"

"I got all the rights I need to take," Longarm told him curtly. "You got some kind of picklock squirreled away, and I aim to find it, even if it makes us miss the train."

For a moment Longarm thought the Kid was going to continue to refuse, but at last the sullen-faced captive shrugged, stood up, and took off his coat, then began unbuttoning his denim shirt. He tossed the discarded garments on the floor, then gestured at his feet.

"You're going to have to take them damn irons off if you want me to step outa my pants," he said sullenly.

"I already figured that out," Longarm replied. "Set down and raise up your feet." He unlocked the ankle-circling cuffs and let them clank to the floor, then stepped back and said, "Go ahead and finish. I want you bare-ass naked."

While the Kid finished undressing, Longarm examined the coat and shirt minutely. He ran his fingers along the seams of both garments, crushed their fabric in his hands, and looked for hidden pockets, but found none. Tossing the coat and shirt back to the Kid, who sat naked on the edge of the bunk, he turned his attention to the underwear and denim trousers. For all his care, he discovered nothing.

"Well, are you satisfied now?" the Kid asked when Longarm threw him the longjohns and trousers.

"Not quite. I still ain't looked at your shoes."

"How could I hide anything in them? Damn it, you can see I don't wear any socks! If I had something hid in my shoes, I'd have a hell of a time walking."

Longarm made no reply. He was spreading open the top of one of the Kid's shoes and running his fingers over their inner lining. The right shoe yielded nothing, but when he explored the left shoe Longarm at last found what he'd been looking for. His fingers encountered a slight bulge in the thin leather lining, and a bit of probing revealed a slit in the leather. After a bit of manipulation, he got the slit open and drew out a strip of steel no thicker than his thumbnail. The metal was finely tempered and flexible, and had been ground to a taper, its tip bent to the shape of an L.

"Just like I figured," Longarm said, tossing the shoe to the floor at the Kid's feet. "I was sure you had this damn picklock tucked away, but I figured it'd be in a place that'd be easier to get to, like a seam in your britches."

"Damn you, Long!" the Stovespit Kid gritted through his clenched teeth. "You're smart, all right, but I'll prove that I'm smarter than you before we're finished!"

"Maybe you will and maybe you won't," Longarm said calmly, tucking the picklock into his wallet. "Now stop your jawing and finish dressing so I can lock them leg irons on you again. Me and you have got a train to catch."

Chapter 13

"You might as well settle in over there by the window," Longarm told the Stovespit Kid, stopping at the back seat of the almost-empty passenger coach and speaking loudly enough to be heard above the wail of the locomotive's signal. The train was about to move.

Whenever he was transporting a prisoner by train, Longarm always chose a seat in the first car behind the baggage car. He had learned that this car was usually the least popular because of a passenger belief going back to a half century earlier, when the railroads first started running.

In the earliest trains, those riding in the first coach were more likely to be killed or injured, and it had become a habit for passengers to avoid that car. Because passengers occupying seats at the front or rear end of a coach were most vulnerable when one of the wooden coaches telescoped, the center seats were considered safer than those at either front or rear.

To isolate a prisoner he was transporting, Longarm's choice had become a rear seat in the first coach. When he entered it from the rear door the car was occupied by only two passengers near its center, and he had stopped at the rearmost seat.

As the Stovespit Kid settled down on the seat nearest the window, a second short whistle blast followed the first. Then the clank of tightening couplings and the rasping of steel wheels on steel rails filled the air, and the coach swayed slightly as it began to move. Through the window the platform of the Sacramento depot seemed momentarily to be moving backward while the eastbound Limited picked up speed.

Since Longarm's quick moves had spoiled his latest effort to escape from the Stockton jail, the Stovespit Kid had remained sullenly silent. During the short trip to Sacramento, he had made no confident boasts, but had shown his frustrated anger by moving more slowly than ever in obeying Longarm's commands and by refusing to talk. Now he slipped across the coach seat like a snail trying to cross a patch of half-dried molasses and settled into place beside the window.

"Spread your knees apart," Longarm said. "I aim to take off one of them leg irons and pass the chain in back of the seat-leg. Then I won't have to worry about you trying to make another getaway by diving out the window."

While the train steadily gained speed across the flat, featureless farmland, Longarm slid the shackle behind the seat-leg and fastened the cuff again around the Kid's ankle. Tossing his saddlebags into the luggage rack above the seat, he settled down and looked across the Kid at the evenly spaced rows of the cornfields that bordered the tracks. Now, at the onset of winter, the stalks were broken, and most of them sagged at unlikely angles between the rows, no longer green, but yellowing or brown.

Out of the corners of his eyes, Longarm took stock of his prisoner. The Stovespit Kid was hunched down in the seat, his arms folded across his chest. His long legs were cramped into an uncomfortable angle, since the chain connecting the leg irons was now too short to allow his feet to reach the footrest attached to the back of the seat ahead. His eyes were closed, his ugly face even uglier than usual because of the frown that creased his forehead and wrinkled the corners of his closed eyes. The frown also set his thick lips in a down-turn that told better than words how he was feeling.

Having decided that there was no way the Kid could manage to escape, Longarm saw no point in trying to make conversation. He slid his hat down over his eyes, leaned back, and wriggled around until he had found the most comfortable position. After a few minutes he dozed, freed from worry and hubbub for the first time since the Kid's escape in Oakland.

Longarm had no idea how long he had been sleeping when the voice of the conductor aroused him. He was awake instantly, pushing his hatbrim back, his eyes going at once to the Stovespit Kid. When he saw that the Kid was still sleeping soundly, Longarm turned to the conductor.

"Sorry I woke you up, Marshal," the trainman apologized. "I didn't realize you were asleep, thought you were just resting your eyes. All I wanted to do was to give you a receipt for your rifle. It's safe in the gun rack up in the baggage coach, and you can pick it up when you get off in Cheyenne."

"You know, that's a damn fool rule," Longarm told the conductor as he took the receipt and tucked it into his vest pocket. "I imagine you'd be right glad I had a rifle where I could put my hand on it if a bunch of train robbers was to pop up someplace down the line."

"You've got a point there, Marshal," the conductor agreed. "I'll bet the brass hats in the head office didn't give a thought to that kind of situation. You might write a letter to them and remind them something like that might happen."

"Maybe I'll do better than just writing a letter myself," Longarm went on thoughtfully. "I'll get my chief to write his boss in Washington about it. He'd wave a bigger stick than somebody can in a job like I got."

"You do that," the conductor said. "Now, I've got to get along and finish up my paperwork. We'll be pulling into Roseville in a few minutes, and it's a pretty busy stop."

After the train pulled out of Roseville, the character of the country began to change as the tracks entered the outskirts of Mother Lode's rolling hills. Longarm had little interest in the scenery. He had crossed the Sierras several times before, and repetition had made this journey routine.

He dozed intermittently as farms gave way to ranches, the ranches to raw land marked only by the trailings of abandoned gold diggings wherever a creek ran. Occasionally the flanks of the constantly steeper hills displayed the monstrous yellow streaks and huge windrows of raw gravel left by the disastrously destructive nozzle of a hydraulic placer mine.

Following the stop at Auburn, the land changed even more rapidly. Both farms and ranches disappeared, and the signs of gold-mining operations vanished. After the train had swayed along for a few more uphill miles, a light, high-hanging haze suddenly blotted out the blue sky and the entire character of the landscape changed. The change became more pronounced in a short time, when it turned into clouds that quickly became heavier and darker. The grades grew steeper and the train's speed slowed perceptibly as the engine puffed more and more laboriously up the western flank of the Sierra Nevadas.

"This damn tin-can train ain't going to make it very much further," the Stovespit Kid remarked unexpectedly.

Longarm looked around in surprise. He had been glancing at the Kid from time to time, whenever he roused from the short naps he'd been enjoying, but every time he had looked, his prisoner had been sleeping.

"I wouldn't worry if I was you," he replied. "We'll be pulling into Truckee in another hour or so, and they'll put on a helper engine to get us over the top hump."

"Hell, I know that, Long. I've made this trip before, you know. Not that I'm worried about how slow we go, or whether we go at all. You wouldn't hear me bellyache if this train was to stop right here and not go any further."

"Now I can understand why you'd feel that way, but we can't go fast enough to suit me," Longarm replied. "I'll be real glad when we get back to Denver and I can turn you over to somebody else to worry about."

An ugly grin twisting his face, the Kid said, "I get the idea you ain't taken to me much."

"I sure ain't, and that's a fact. Shut up now and let me go back to sleep."

"Like I said, I've just about caught up on the shuteye I've missed," the Kid went on, ignoring Longarm's suggestion. "I don't feel like sleeping any longer."

"Turn around and look out the window, then," Longarm told him in a flat voice. "I'd a sight rather doze than look at you."

"Hell, there's not going to be anything to look at in a little while," the Kid said. "It's starting to snow."

Glancing past the Stovespit Kid, Longarm saw that the air was now filled with whirling white flakes. He peered ahead and saw that on the steep slope the train was now mounting the snow had already covered the ground.

"Likely it's just a little early-winter drizzle," he said. "It won't be much at this time of the year. I've been over this

119

stretch of track two or three times before at this time of the year and never run into anything really bad."

This time the Kid made no effort to continue the conversation. He was staring out the window at the swirling snowflakes which were growing thicker as the train continued its slow progress up the steep grade.

Only a short time earlier, at a lower altitude than they had now reached, the snow had melted as fast as it struck the ground. However, along the stretch of track they were just entering, it was clinging. White tufts formed on the pines that grew densely on the sharply angled slope, and a thin coating of tiny flakes capped the tops of the boulders that had begun to break through the spare layer of soil as the altitude increased.

Occasionally now the coach in which Longarm and the Kid were riding jerked and slipped backward when the locomotive encountered a stretch of track where the snow had frozen on the steel rails and formed a thin coating of ice. The wind had increased in velocity at the higher altitude, and the snow was no longer falling in small flakes that came straight down. The white stuff was swirling outside the coach windows, occasionally sticking to the glass panes in patches that clung briefly before being snatched away by the wind.

"Damned if I don't think we're running into a real storm," Longarm commented as he peered past the Kid at the scene outside the window.

"That's what I've been trying to tell you." The Stovespit Kid did not turn his eyes away from the pane. "And that bucket of bolts this damn railroad calls an engine sounds like it's really having trouble."

Before Longarm could reply, the coach quivered and came to a slow halt. The chugging of the locomotive increased in intensity. Then the train began to move slowly backward.

Its reverse slide did not last long. A high-pitched metallic grating drifted back to the coach as the engineer opened the sandboxes that were fixed ahead of and behind the engine's massive drive wheels. The backward slide slowed and halted, and a pulsing shook the entire train as the engineer shoved his throttle forward. The sliding wheels grated on the sanded rails and found traction again, and the train once more moved ahead.

Progress was slow for a few moments. Then the cars began to sway as the engine picked up speed. Looking past the Kid out the window, Longarm saw that the snow now stood a foot deep beside the tracks. The pines were thinner here, and through the heavy snowfall he could see the trees as conical snow-shrouded shapes standing in dark cups of snow. The ground surrounding the tree trunks was visible beneath the low-hanging bottom branches, and he could tell that the snow now stood more than a foot deep.

By now the train was moving ahead once more. Progress was slow but steady as the train passed through a stretch where some vagary of the sharply upslanted terrain had caused the snow to fall less heavily. The respite from the storm was brief, however. After a few miles of slowed but uninterrupted progress the track curved through the section of almost-bare ground, and the grade grew steeper and the snowfall heavier.

High drifts reappeared. Looking through the window, Longarm saw that in places the bottom branches of the smaller pines were completely buried. Against the boles of bigger trees the snow had piled in narrow triangular drifts to the height of a tall man's chest.

"This ain't no little bitty snowfall," he commented. "Looks to me like we've run into a real big storm."

"Yep," the Stovespit Kid agreed without turning his eyes away from the window. "And the higher we climb, the worse it's going to get."

"We'll make it into Truckee, all right," Longarm went on confidently. "As I recall, there's snowsheds sheltering the tracks in the worst spots just a little ways ahead, and old Crocker was smart enough to build more of 'em all the way over Donner Pass. Once we get over this hump, it'll be clear going till we run into the Rockies between Cheyenne and Denver."

"That might just be some time from now." The Kid's voice was flat. "Look what we're running into up ahead."

Looking through the window ahead of their seat, Longarm

saw that a big snowdrift had formed slantwise across the tracks. The drift was visible only faintly through the heavy downfall of still more white flakes.

These were not the small, dry flakes they had encountered at a lower altitude. They were thick, wet blobs that struck the windows and clung for several moments until heat from inside the car seeped through the glass and softened the flakes. Then the wind created by the train's motion sent them sliding back to the edge of the windows, where they merged with an earlier icy accumulation that was already five or six inches wide.

Suddenly the noise of the locomotive grew louder and became a minor roll of thunder. The coach was plunged into darkness as it entered the first snowshed. While it passed through the shed, a structure like an inverted L with its roof anchored in a solid granite cliff and its protecting wall shielding the tracks, the coach stayed dark. Then the train emerged into the white landscape once more.

While passing through the shed, the engine had picked up speed on the clear stretch of track. Though the drifts it hit when leaving the snowshed were higher than any it had encountered before, it had gained enough momentum passing through the shed with its clear stretch of track to plow through the clinging piled-up snow. It pushed the drifts aside without trouble, though with the aid of an almost constant stream of sand, until it came to the next snowshed.

Once more the drumming and the darkness took over for a few minutes as the train picked up speed again moving through the protecting structure which covered the tracks, and it pushed through the next stretch of drifts without trouble. It moved easily through the third snowshed and the drifts that were piled ahead of its exit, even though the grade was noticeably steeper.

Then, on a sweeping curve which the train entered after leaving the third shed, the weather finally defeated the engine. It plowed into a massive drift that towered like a white cliff even higher than the smokestack, plunged into the sloping wall of snow, and ground to a stop, its wheels still spinning.

Slowly, with a great huffing and puffing, the train began backing out of the drift. It backed for almost a mile before the engineer braked, then started ahead again. The train gained speed quickly. It covered the half-mile of track and pounded into the wall of snow, driving into the hole it had cleared in the drift on its first effort and pushed the snow aside for almost a dozen yards. Then it stopped for the second time, its boiler buried to the engine cab, before grinding to a shrill, shrieking halt as the massive drive wheels fought vainly for traction.

"Just like I told you," the Stovespit Kid said to Longarm, satisfaction in his voice. "It looks like this is as far as we're going until the snow melts."

"I wouldn't be too sure about that," Longarm replied. "We ain't but a few miles from Truckee now, and it's a division point, if I recall correctly. When the train don't show up there on time, they'll send a snowplow to clear the tracks."

"By the time the plow gets here, we'll all be frozen," the Kid retorted. "It's already getting cold in here."

Longarm realized the truth of his statement. With the locomotive halted, the excess steam from its boiler that circulated through the passenger coaches had stopped. The small potbelly stove that stood in the front of the coach still threw out heat, but not enough to keep the car comfortably warm. Though only a short time had passed since the train had stopped, the coach was already growing chilly and the windows were beginning to be obscured by a coating of frost.

"Was I you, I wouldn't worry too much about freezing," Longarm told the Kid. "I ain't been in this kind of fix before, but it's dollars to doughnuts the train crew has. They'll figure out a way to keep that stove working."

"They damn well better!" the Kid retorted. "It ain't my idea to be here in the first place, you know."

"Even if you wanted to, there ain't much of a place you could run to," Longarm pointed out. "And I—" He broke off as the conductor came in carrying a scuttle full of coal. The trainman's eyes flicked over the passenger seats and stopped on Longarm. He jerked his head in a beckoning gesture. Longarm went on, "I guess I better go see what he wants."

Getting up, Longarm walked to the front of the coach. When Longarm was within earshot, the conductor said, "I

123

hope you don't mind doing me a favor, Marshal Long."

"Anything within reason, I'll be glad to help out."

"Take charge of this stove, if you don't mind," the conductor said. "We usually get a helper engine at the siding in Soda Springs, and don't have to worry about running short of coal. But we've used up a lot bucking the drifts and trying to keep up speed, so we're pretty much scraping bottom right now. If you'd just keep an eye on this stove and keep the passengers from wasting coal, I'd be real obliged."

"Glad to," Longarm said. Then he asked, "How long do you think we're going to be stuck here?"

"That's hard to say. The head brakeman could probably tell you, though. He went out as soon as we stopped to climb a pole and send a message to the division point at Truckee, telling them to hurry up with a snowplow and the helper loco."

"He'd be up with the engineer, then, I reckon?" When the conductor nodded, Longarm went on, "Maybe I better go up and find out. Not that I could do anything to help, but I'm sorta curious about what running late the way we are is going to do to my connections into Denver."

"What about your prisoner?"

"Oh, he'll stay put. I got him in leg irons, and they're looped around a seat-leg."

Longarm pushed through the front coach door and into the vestibule, where the cold struck him like a fist. Hurrying into the deserted baggage car to stay out of the chill as long as possible, he squeezed along the narrow clear strip beside the tender and swung up into the engine cab. The engineer, fireman, and head brakeman were standing as close to the boiler as they could get, their heads close together. They looked around when Longarm stepped into the cab.

"Something wrong?" the engineer asked. "If there is, you'll have to find the conductor and tell him about it."

"Nothing's wrong except what everybody already knows about," Longarm replied. "And the conductor's the one that sent me up here. I'm a United States marshal, and I got a prisoner that I'm taking back to Denver I was just wondering what stopping this way's going to do to my train connection in Cheyenne."

"If we're lucky, we'll make up lost time between here and Cheyenne," the engineer replied. "If we don't, you might have to lay over there a few hours."

"Well, that sure ain't going to kill me," Longarm said. "I don't suppose you can make a guess how long we'll be stuck here?"

"Not a chance. That's going to depend on how long it'll take for the snowplow to clear the tracks for our helper."

"I sorta figured that," Longarm said. "Well, I'll mosey on back and settle down till we get started again."

Hurrying back through the biting cold that struck him with increased intensity after he left the warm engine cab, Longarm hurried through the baggage car and into the passenger coach. He was halfway down the aisle before he realized that the seat which had been occupied by his prisoner was vacant. Not quite believing what he had seen, he flicked his eyes along the aisle.

The Stovespit Kid had simply disappeared.

Chapter 14

For a moment Longarm stood in frozen astonishment, staring at the vacant seat. Instinctively, he turned his eyes toward the window, but the coating of frost on the pane shut off his view of the outside. There were only two other passengers in the coach, both of them drummers. They had created space to sort their orders and notes by reversing the backs of the seats in front of them to provide a place where they could work. Longarm stopped between them.

"That fellow sitting by me in the back seat," he said, taking both of them into his question by looking from one to the other. "Did you men see him get off?"

"I wasn't paying any attention," one of them said. "I was busy with my paperwork."

"So was I," the other told him. "I guess he decided he'd rather sit in one of the other cars."

With a nod of thanks, Longarm turned and walked back to the rear of the car, mulling over the first riddle that had popped into his mind.

There wasn't no way on earth the Stovespit Kid could've slipped a foot outa one of them shackles, he told himself. *And he sure couldn't't've slid under the seat and skinned through the legs, because there ain't more'n two or three inches of room between the seat bottom and the floor. And them legs is iron, so he couldn't't've busted one without he had a hammer, which he didn't, because there's no place he could've got hold of one.*

By this time he had reached the seats he and the Kid had occupied. Bending over the green plush cushions, he examined them closely. At this first quick look they seemed to be in order. Then he noticed that the seat which the Stovespit Kid had occupied seemed to be slightly canted. He prodded it experimentally, and the seat settled a fraction of an inch, then stopped with a click of metal against metal. The cushioned pad was once again level.

"Now what in hell did I do?" Longarm asked himself under his breath.

Dropping to his knees, he leaned forward and explored the legs and seat bottom with his fingers. In less than a minute he found the answer to what had seemed an impossible riddle.

Though the coach seat appeared to be a single unit, it was actually made in three separate parts: legs, seat, and back. Both the legs and the hinges that allowed the back to be reversed were attached firmly to the floor by big screws, but the seat was built on a square frame of metal that had a short stub of tubing extending from the bottom of the frame at each corner. The tubing simply slipped down over the top of the legs and was held in place by thumb-screws.

In a flash, Longarm understood how his prisoner had managed to escape. Earlier in the trip, while Longarm was sleeping after the train left Sacramento, the Stovespit Kid must have discovered the method by which the seats were assembled. Gambling that Longarm would not wake up, and that at some time during the trip he would be left alone, the Kid had loosened the thumb-screws. When Longarm went forward to talk to the engine crew, he had simply pulled the seat off the legs and lifted the chain connecting the leg irons over the seat-leg.

That Stovespit Kid's a lot smarter than you been giving him credit for being, old son, Longarm told himself as he dropped the seat back into place. *Chances are this ain't the first time he's made a slick getaway off a train by pulling this very stunt! But he ain't free yet. He's got outa the seat, all right, but he can't get rid of them leg irons quite so easy. And he ain't damn fool enough to go out in this storm. Likely he's found a hidey-hole somewhere on this train, and all you'll have to do is dig him out.*

Longarm wasted no time in beginning his search. The restrooms were at the rear of the car, just behind the seats he and

127

the Kid had occupied, and he made them his first target. He opened the door of the men's room and found it empty, as was the ladies' room across the aisle. Working toward the end of the train, paying no attention to the startled stares of the passengers when they saw him open a door marked "Ladies," Longarm checked each car in turn.

The Kid was not in any of them.

Well, he sure as hell wouldn't've gone up front toward the engine, because he'd know he'd run into me, Longarm told himself thoughtfully. *Maybe he shinnied up on top of one of the cars or ducked under 'em. If he was fool enough to do that, he'd be froze enough to give up by now, so the next thing is to take a look-see and find out.*

When Longarm stepped into the vestibule, the cold struck him like a giant fist that bombarded every square inch of exposed skin with its icy chill. Slitting his eyelids against the cold, he looked down at the surface of the snow below the car's steps. Deep oval holes showed where the Stovespit Kid had jumped off the bottom step and started away from the train.

Longarm lifted his eyes and scanned the white expanse that stretched away from the rails. The line of identations leading away from the train marked the path the Kid had taken, but the snow was still falling heavily, whirling in the bone-cutting wind.

Gazing through the whirling flakes until his eyes had grown accustomed to the snowfall and to the glare that rose from the white ground-cover, Longarm's eyes followed the shadowy trail left by the Stovespit Kid's feet as they had poked through the fresh snow. After several moments he caught sight of the Kid again, a small dark figure against the white landscape and the brown tree trunks. Even at that distance he could see that the Kid was having trouble making headway.

That poor damn fool! Longarm thought. For a moment, his instinctive sympathy with anyone in the sort of plight the Kid had created for himself overcame his distaste for the fugitive as an individual. *Likely he won't get very far. He ain't dressed to be out in this kind of weather, and them leg irons won't help him none. But you ain't dressed too damn warm either, old son, and you ain't got no choice but to do your duty and go after him, whether you like it or not.*

Longarm stood in the vestibule watching the Stovespit Kid's painfully slow progress. He knew that there was no need for him to hurry. Hampered by the leg irons, buffeted by the freezing wind that whistled down the slope from the crest of the Sierra Nevadas, the Stovespit Kid was not going far. And no matter how much distance he covered, his prints in the snow would remain as a trail. Suddenly realizing that he'd started shivering in the arctic air, Longarm stepped back into the coach.

Picking up his saddlebags, Longarm walked briskly to the baggage car. The entire train crew was gathered around the little pot-bellied stove that stood in the center of the car and created a small oasis of heat.

"I got to get my rifle," he told the baggagemaster. "That damn fool prisoner I'm taking back to Denver's give me the slip. He's already a quarter of a mile away, and I don't aim to give him no more of a head start than he's got now."

"You can't stay outside long in this kind of weather, Marshal!" the conductor protested. Looking at Longarm's serge coat, he went on, "That coat won't cut the cold. You'll freeze!"

"Then I'll just be froze," Longarm replied, going to the rack that held his Winchester and lifting off the rifle. "If push comes to shove, you men don't look like you're much better off than I am, and it's my job to keep that fellow from getting clean away."

"Can you get him back by the time we're ready to roll again?" the engineer asked. "The snowplow's going to be here in the next half-hour, and I can't hold the train for you."

"I ain't asking you to," Longarm replied. "I don't know how long it'll take me to catch up with him, but if I miss getting back before you start, I'll take him into the closest town and catch tomorrow's train."

"Truckee's the nearest place you can head for," the conductor told him. "And you won't have any trouble keeping to the road. Even if it's nothing but a sorta trail, the stagecoach outfit's cut down a bunch of trees to straighten it out on the worst grades, and the stumps will mark it out as plain as a row of fenceposts would."

"How far is it from here to Truckee?" Longarm asked.

"Ten, maybe twelve miles. You'll have a lot of zigzagging to do getting up to Donner Pass, but once you make it there the rest of the way's all downhill."

"If it'll help you any, there's a couple of logging camps between here and Truckee," the brakeman volunteered. "They're off the road a ways, but they'll stand out like sore thumbs in this snow. You won't have too much trouble finding them."

"I don't guess they're cutting timber at this time of year?" Longarm asked.

"No, but you can shelter in one of the bunkhouses if you don't make it back before we roll," the trainman replied. "Up here, they don't lock up the camps when they shut down, because once winter sets in nobody can get to 'em."

"That's good to know," Longarm said. "I thank you kindly. Now, I better start moving before that prisoner gets too much of a lead on me."

"Wait a minute!" the baggagemaster broke in. "We've got a half-dozen sheepskin coats hanging on that rack over there, just for this kind of weather. I don't think the railroad would object if I loaned you one of them."

"You'll be needing them coats for yourselves, if you got to do any outside work when that snowplow and helper engine get here," Longarm said. "I wouldn't feel right about it."

"Don't worry about us," the conductor told him. He stepped over to the rack and took down one of the coats. "We won't have much outside work to do in getting rolling." He handed Longarm the coat. "Just leave it with the stationmaster at Truckee or Reno, and I'll pick it up next time we're through."

Longarm took the heavy fleece-lined coat and hefted it. He said, "I sure won't turn it down, and I thank you kindly for your help." He was slipping the coat on as he spoke. "Now I got to get on my way."

For the first hundred yards he covered after struggling up

the steep, slanting sides of the railroad grade, Longarm had little trouble. Though the snow was still falling fairly heavily, the tracks left by the Stovespit Kid were unmistakable, for the leg irons had limited him to short, careful steps and the chain that connected the shackles had cut a deep groove between the oval depressions left by his feet.

Longarm took long strides along the trail the Kid had left, the snow squeaking as his feet sank into it. As minutes piled on minutes, the chill of the knee-deep snow began to numb his feet. He tried to stamp them on the ground to warm them, but the snow cushioned his boot soles.

Best thing you can do is just keep moving, he told himself, his eyes focused steadily on the dark blob to which the swirling flakes reduced the figure of the Stovespit Kid. *It ain't much consolation, but he's a lot worse off than you are, old son.*

Ahead of him, on the steadily uptilting ground, the fugitive was still moving. As Longarm moved higher up the slope the trees were spaced farther apart, and he had less trouble keeping the Kid in sight. The snow was not falling as heavily as it had been, and the storm seemed to be tapering down.

Behind the grey clouds that covered the sky, Longarm could see an area of concentrated glow that marked the position of the sun. It was dropping toward the west, and he estimated that he had another three hours of daylight left in which to close the gap between him and his quarry. Shrugging his shoulders to settle the borrowed coat a little more comfortably, he slogged doggedly onward.

Longarm could not be sure of the exact moment when he lost sight of the Stovespit Kid. All he knew was that he had seen the small black blur he was following before a vagrant wind picked up some of the surface snow and whirled it in a cloud that blocked his view. The air was clouded for perhaps ten minutes, and when the blown snow moved on or sifted down once more, the Kid was no longer visible.

Baffled, Longarm stopped and peered ahead for several seconds, looking for what had by now become a familiar sight. The passage of the eddying wind had left the air relatively clear. He could make out the trees ahead quite easily,

131

but there was no black blob moving along among them.

Maybe he stopped and sat down to rest, he told himself silently. *Or maybe he got tired and figured he'd lean up against one of the trees to take a breather. One thing's for sure, he couldn't get noplace any faster than he's been moving, and there ain't anywhere he can hide. He's got to be hid by one of them big trees, or maybe down in a gully that'd hide him.*

Suddenly Longarm became aware that he had no sensation at all in his own feet. He stopped and stamped them for a few minutes until they began tingling and prickling again, then resumed his steady forward progress, guided by the craters which the feet of the Stovespit Kid had formed.

By now the bite of the thin, sharp air in this high altitude was beginning to affect even Longarm's well-conditioned physique. Each time he inhaled, his throat and lungs protested with a sharp pang. His feet were without feeling. His rifle felt heavier, even though he had been shifting it at intervals from one hand to the other, and the saddlebags over his shoulder seemed to be dragging at him and making him walk lopsided.

Just ahead of him, Longarm noticed a bigger, taller pine tree than most, one of those giants of the forests that are to be found in almost every stand of lesser pines. As he drew closer to the imposing forest giant, he noticed that the widely spreading lower branches had kept the swirling snow from falling in a narrow belt around its bole. The snow-free circle was only a foot or so wide, and was covered with a layer of pine needles, but it was the first clear spot he had seen since leaving the train. He ducked below the bottom branches and slid down to the clear area.

After having been in snow constantly from the beginning of his pursuit, Longarm was instantly aware that the ground below his boot soles felt almost warm. A convenient fork offered a place to hold his rifle, the snag of a broken twig a place to hang his saddlebags. His hands and arms free, Longarm stood erect and stretched, his head between the tree's lowest limbs.

Though the branches overhead shielded him from the snowflakes that kept drifting down, the chill of the air seemed

132

more intense now that he was no longer moving. Sliding his stiff, cold hand between the top buttons of his sheepskin coat, Longarm managed to fumble a cigar and a match out of his vest pocket. He scraped his thumbnail across the match-head and puffed until the long, thin cheroot was drawing to his satisfaction. The grey smoke he exhaled roiled in the cold air like a miniature cloud before dissipating in the green snow-flecked branches.

A train whistle broke the silence with its mournful wail. Longarm shifted his feet until he could look back down the long slope. He saw the white plumes sent up by the snowplow on the railroad tracks, now far below him. The plow was followed by the helper locomotive, running tender ahead.

He watched while the plow nosed into the passenger train, the helper following at once. The three engines huffed steam for a moment, then started ahead, dragging the passenger train behind them. In a moment they vanished behind the high drifts lining the tracks.

Looks like it's shank's mare for you on into Truckee, old son, he told himself silently. *But that won't be till you've corraled that damn Stovespit Kid, which you ain't going to do if you stand here like a moonstruck calf any longer.*

Longarm shouldered his saddlebags, then took his rifle from the tree. He was careful to grab it low on the waist of its stock, for he'd long ago learned that if his bare skin touched the metal of a weapon exposed very long to such freezing cold, the skin would adhere to the metal and be stripped away when the gun was released. Bending low and dodging the low branches of the tree, he stamped his way up to the level and took up his pursuit again.

There was no sign of the Stovespit Kid when he searched the terrain ahead with his eyes, but the marks of the fugitive's feet were still plainly visible. Longarm followed them up the slope. Its angle grew steeper until he could see the bare rocks as dark blobs against the snowdrifts that now formed a regular peak with only the tops of trees and the clouded sky ahead. The footprints led him to the crest, where a jagged U-shaped break marked the place where the Kid had passed before him.

At the top of the ridge, the snow was unstable and shifting

underfoot. Longarm looked down at the stagecoach road the train conductor had mentioned, and the heavily forested slope beyond. There were no wheel ruts on the curving expanse of road visible from his vantage point, but close-spaced footprints, which could only belong to the Stovespit Kid, broke its smooth surface. The prints were in the center of the road and led up the grade to Donner Pass.

Longarm slid down the grade and followed them.

Chapter 15

There ain't nothing like trying to stay outa jail that'll give a man the craw to hike up this kind of a road in this kind of weather, old son, Longarm told himself. Just then his feet slipped on another patch of ice that had been hidden under the snow and he was forced to flail his arms wildly to keep from falling. *From what I seen of the Stovespit Kid, he didn't have that kind of nerve, but I guess all he can think about is that hangman's rope he's got waiting for him if he don't get away.*

Since he had started up the steep grade more than two miles back, Longarm's progress to Donner Summit had been one of constant struggle. While the stagecoach road was free of such obstructions as trees, it wound in sharp curves to avoid the massive boulders that broke the snow's surface on both sides. The huge monoliths rose above Longarm's head, their domed tops capped with white, their downcurving flanks a sullen grey, two or three shades darker than the snowcaps.

Underfoot, the road's surface was rutted by the wheels of the vehicles that had used it and the snows that had swept over the pass before the present storm had turned it into a solid layer of ice under its covering of new flakes. The slant of the ground had grown progressively steeper, and the cold had stiffened the leather soles of Longarm's boots. The boot soles were no longer flexible, but as rigid and hard as thick metal sheets on which the ice-slick leather skidded in unpredictable fashion.

A quarter of a mile ahead of him, Longarm could see the top of the pass, the place where the slope ended abuptly and beyond it nothing showed except the gray, darkening sky. The heart of the storm had passed and moved on while he had been struggling up the pass. There were only a few flakes falling now, but the cold had increased. Each breath Longarm took brought a stabbing chill into his lungs and his mouth was dry in spite of his efforts to create saliva by swallowing frequently.

Longarm could tell from the evidence of the Stovespit Kid's tracks that the fugitive was in worse shape than he was himself. The Kid's footprints had grown more and more erratic, and twice Longarm had encountered the imprint of his body in the soft surface snow, marking spots where the Kid had fallen face down.

He's bound to be tired by now, Longarm frowned when he came across another place where the snow gave evidence of a fall and showed the streaked criss-cross marks of the Kid's hands where he had clawed the snow in his efforts to beg back to his feet. *He sure as hell can't last much longer. You oughta be catching sight of him any minute now.*

In spite of the assurances he gave himself, Longarm did not see the Stovespit Kid as he began his descent of the pass. Going down the steep, rocky incline was even more of a task than climbing to its summit had been. The road's surface under its mask of snow seemed even more slippery than before, and keeping his feet under him was an even more difficult task. Although long streaks on the snow's surface told Longarm that the Stovespit Kid had encountered the same problem, it was small consolation.

"Whoever called this damn streak of ice a road was sure playing fast and loose with his language," Longarm muttered under his breath as he skidded to a halt and relaxed after a long session of flailing his arms to avoid falling. "A man don't need boots on his feet when he's trying to stay on 'em on a road like this one. What'd be more like it is a pair of ice skates."

He started moving again, but had taken only a dozen steps when his feet hit a new streak of ice below the snow. This time no amount of arm-swinging helped. Longarm fell, and began skidding on his back down the precipitous incline. His slide covered twenty yards before the ice beneath the snow gave way to a path of rough earth. Even though the dirt was frozen as hard as the granite where he had originally fallen, the rough clods of soil slowed his momentum, and by using the rifle butt as a brake he was able to stop himself.

Longarm did not get to his feet at once, but sat quietly in spite of the chill that was swiftly creeping from his buttocks to his thighs. He dug out a cigar and lighted it, looking back at the streak his slide had left in the steep incline. Shaking his head, he used the butt of his rifle to lever himself to his feet and resumed his descent of the pass.

Longarm had covered a hundred yards or more, feeling his way with greater care now, before he realized with a start that he had seen no signs of the Stovespit Kid's passing since his fall. He stopped and looked back up the slope. About midway down the long streak left on the snow's surface by his slide, he saw what his fall had caused him to miss: the Kid's footprints, where his quarry had left the road and angled off through the pines.

Now why the hell would he do a fool thing like that? Longarm asked himself silently as he studied the path the Kid had left in the virgin surface of the snow-covered ground. *There ain't nothing that way except trees. But that smart little son of a bitch must've seen something you didn't, old son, or he'd still be making tracks towards Truckee.*

Shaking his head, Longarm started up the grade toward the fresh trail left by his quarry. Before he was within a dozen yards of the Kid's unexpected trail, Longarm found the reason he had been seeking. Through the thick-standing trunks of the pines down the slope from the road he saw the black bulk of several buildings.

Now, that's got to be one of them logging stands the train conductor told you about, he thought. *And you didn't see it because you was going a hundred miles an hour, sliding on your butt when you went by. Chances are, when you get to them buildings you're going to find the Kid holed up in one of 'em.*

Plodding through the knee-deep drifts created by air swirls around the stand of pines, Longarm angled down the slope toward the trees. Some twenty yards after he had left the road, he came again to the trail left by the Stovespit Kid. He had followed it for less than half a mile before the forest ended abruptly. For almost a mile in all directions there were no more trees, only a forest of stumps rising from the snow, surrounded by a sea of hummocks. The two buildings were only fifty or sixty yards away now, and the Kid's footprints led directly to the largest.

Longarm wasted no time in ducking behind the closest stump and hunkering down while he took stock of his position. He had spent enough time in lumbering country to read the signs left on the land around him. He recognized the snow-covered humps as slash-piles, where the loggers had trimmed the felled trees of their branches, and he was reasonably sure of what he would find inside the buildings. He planned his approach to take advantage of the stumps and heaps of trimmings.

Picking his way around the slash-piles, he dodged from one stump to the next until less than twenty feet separated him from the larger of the two buildings.

Oozing sap from the fresh-cut stumps had frozen into streaks and bubbles on the tops of the raw stumps, and glistened like amber in the fading daylight. The two buildings were of raw-sawn pine, and they, too, were streaked with amber sap. One of the structures was little more than a shed, and as Longarm drew closer he could see a steam boiler on a shelf shovelled out of the slanting ground.

Between the small shedlike building and its larger, more solidly built counterpart, the dark line of a little creek meandered through the snow. In the otherwise unbroken surface of the snow covering the clearing, close-spaced dark spots marked the path the Stovespit Kid had made as he explored the area, and Longarm traced the Kid's footprints with his eyes.

From where Longarm had taken cover, the footprints showed that the Kid had gone directly to the larger building. A second set of prints led to the shed. There was a third set leading away from the shed, back to the large building, and a fourth line of prints that angled from it across the little clearing and through the stump-covered area that extended for a hundred yards or more, to the point where the virgin forest began again. As he studied the spacing of this last set of prints, a frown began wrinkling Longarm's forehead.

"Damned if that Stovespit Kid didn't manage to get free from them leg irons," he muttered under his breath. "He's walking free again, no two ways about it. And counting all that time I was fool enough to waste before I took after him, he's likely got at least a two-hour lead by now, maybe as much as three. But he's bound to be real tired, and by rights he'd oughta stopped here to rest up, even stay the night, except it's real plain he didn't, for some reason or other."

Satisfied that his slippery quarry had lived up to his nickname again, Longarm left the cover of the pine bole and walked to the larger of the two buildings. The low rectangular structure had no windows. When he rounded the corner he could see its door hanging ajar on a pair of makeshift leather hinges.

Wasting no more time, Longarm went inside. The interior was gloomy and as Longarm's eyes adjusted to the dismal light he saw that it contained only a table, a pot-bellied sheet-iron stove, and a few chairs clustered around it. Bunks lined both the back wall and the wall at one end, wisps of straw protruding from their thin canvas-covered mattresses. Shelves stacked with heavy crockery plates and cups took up half the wall at the opposite end, and an assortment of skillets, pots, and pans hung beside the shelves, close to the stove.

Looks like whoever was working this logging camp figures to come back in the spring, Longarm thought as he scanned the room. *Just walked away and left everything the way it is when that first snowfall started, most likely. Can't say I blame 'em, either. Nobody's apt to stop by here after the snow piles up a little bit, and it won't be long before these buildings is plumb covered up.*

Satisfied that time spent in a closer examination would be wasted, Longarm dropped his saddlebags inside the door and followed the Kid's footprints to the shed. A quick glance told him all he needed to know. A forge and a large anvil took up half the interior. A few rusted and broken blades of two-man felling-saws were strewn on the dirt floor. Nails driven into the wall showed where tools had been hung, though no tools were in sight except a large hammer with a broken handle that lay on the anvil.

"That's the answer, then," Longarm said to himself.

He stepped over to the anvil and picked up the hammer. Its ends were marred, but the bright streaks on its head that gleamed between the scars showed it had been used very recently. Looking in the loose dirt underfoot, Longarm saw several strips of shining metal and bent to pick up one of them. He had his hand on one when he saw a link of chain, bent and almost shapeless, the only clue to its identity the ragged, shining ends.

Longarm picked it up, together with two or three of the metal strips. The strips were bent and twisted, but their origin was unmistakable. They had come from one of the pieces of discarded two-man saws. The piece of steel was bent and twisted, one end flattened by repeated blows of the hammer, and what was left of its teeth on the other end shattered and broken, leaving a chisel-sharp jagged edge. The chain-link was twisted almost beyond recognition, but he could see by the raggedness of the ends that many, many blows of the hammer on the saw-strips had at last weakened it until it could be twisted and broken.

It's plain as day, all right, he thought. *The Stovespit Kid sure ain't no kinda damn fool. Steel that's good enough to go into a big saw like these pieces come from would be just about as good as a chisel to bust through a link of that chain. First he was smart enough to get away from the train, now he's got his legs free.*

Letting the strips of steel fall back to the floor, Longarm started back to the bunkhouse. The eastern sky was growing dark now and the snow was swirling down thickly once more. The clouds still hung low and threatened a heavy snowfall during the night. He reached the bunkhouse, went inside, and dropped into the nearest chair.

There ain't no way of telling how long it taken the Kid to bust that chain, he told himself. *But one thing's sure, he lost a lot of time, and he ain't so far ahead now. Course, he'll move faster now that he's got his legs free, but that ain't such a never mind, because in another half-hour or so it's going to be pitch dark.*

Now, there ain't no way you can keep tracking the Kid once daylight's gone, he told himself. *He's smart enough to figure that out, and he'll be smart enough to know he ain't got no more chance than a snowball in hell of living through the night unless he shelters someplace, so he's bound to hole up. He sure won't be no further ahead of you tomorrow morning at daybreak than he is about now, so you better hole up, too, right here in this bunkhouse where you ain't going to freeze to death.*

His decision made, Longarm wasted no time. He went outside and attacked the nearest slash-pile. It yielded enough small half-dry branches with withered pine needles still clinging to them to keep him in firewood for the night. The air was growing steadily colder in the gathering darkness, and Longarm hurriedly dragged the branches to the big bunkhouse. When he had made three trips, he was sure he had enough firewood for the night. He chose a double handful of twigs with the driest needles, closed the door, and in the gloom of the windowless bunkhouse he kindled a fire in the stove.

Grudgingly, the cold air gave up its grip on the interior of the barnlike structure. Longarm busied himself while waiting for the room to warm by bringing in enough branches from the heap he had dragged up to keep the stove stoked up through the night. Darkness came on suddenly, as it does at high altitudes, and in the warm room Longarm quickly grew drowsy.

He fixed himself a bed in one of the bunks. By emptying two of the sacklike mattresses and transferring the shredded straw left in them to a third, he made a passable mattress. By the time he had finished, the interior was warm enough for him to take off the sheepskin coat. Spreading the coat over the mattress for cover, he folded his coat for a pillow, then pulled a chair over beside the stove and sat down in the warm glow it cast to smoke a final cheroot.

Somehow, the familiar action had a soothing effect on the protests of his empty stomach. When he had smoked the cigar to a stub he unbuckled his gunbelt, placed his Colt on a chair beside the bunk where it would be handy to reach during the night, and leaned his rifle on the chair. Levering off his boots, he crawled into the bunk, folded his long legs, and pulled the sheepskin coat over him. Within two minutes he was asleep.

Protesting rumbles from his empty stomach woke Longarm. He had gotten up twice during the night to replenish the fire, but since the last time he had added wood the sap-heavy pieces of pine had burned away to ashes and the bunkhouse was growing cold. Swinging out of the bunk, he tossed the last of the firewood onto the few coals that remained in the pot-bellied stove.

As the fresh fuel brought the fire back to life, he fumbled in his vest pocket for his watch. The hands showed the hour to be five. Yawning and stretching, Longarm forced his feet into his boots and finished dressing. His empty stomach had not stopped its rumbling, but he ignored it. Buckling on his gunbelt, he shrugged into the sheepskin coat and threw his saddlebags over his shoulder. Picking up his rifle, he stepped out the door, where the icy air struck him like a club.

Very little more snow had fallen during the night, only a thin sprinkling of fresh flakes. The clouds had passed on, and in the brightening sky the stars were retreating before the oncoming sunrise. There was enough light for Longarm to see the snow-blurred edges of the footprints made by the Stovespit Kid when he had left the logging stand the evening before. They formed a straight line leading toward the untouched forest beyond the cutover area.

There ain't all that much light, old son, Longarm told himself silently as he gazed at the grey line of dawn that showed on the jagged horizon. *But there's enough to keep from missing the Kid's tracks. And it ought not be long before you catch up with him, if you hustle.*

Longarm started following the snow-dusted depressions. In the before-sunrise chill, the snow crust crunched under his boot soles as he crossed the logged-over area toward the line of untouched pines a quarter of a mile away. On his left the land sloped gently down. On his right the line of jagged rock marking the crest of Donner Summit was outlined sharply against the sky, which was now pink with the promise of sunrise.

Except for the crisp crunching of Longarm's boot soles as they cracked through the snow-crust, no sound broke the morning stillness. He had covered half the distance to the line of uncut pines before his stomach started growling again. He stopped and rested his rifle against his thigh while sliding a hand into his vest pocket to take out a cigar and a match.

Before his hand reached his vest pocket a rifle cracked from the trees ahead. The slug whined past Longarm's head as he dropped flat. His saddlebags flew off his shoulder and tumbled into the snow a yard ahead of him. Lying prone, Longarm reached for his own. rifle, which had slid off his thigh when he moved. A second report cracked from the pines and the bullet kicked up a puff of snow a foot away from him.

Longarm had his hand on the barrel of his own rifle by now. He shouldered the weapon while his eyes searched vainly for a target in the darkness that shrouded the pines in front of him.

Chapter 16

Longarm lay motionless, his eyes flicking along the dark boles of the trees that sheltered the hidden sniper. The sunrise sky was bright above the top of the trees, the sun's rim visible between their spiked tips, the trunks lying in deep shadow.

That's got to be the Stovespit Kid, he reasoned. *But how in hell did he get his hands on a gun?*

He searched vainly for some sign of motion in the trees. Several minutes passed, minutes that seemed twice as long as usual, and as they ticked away Longarm decided to use the oldest trick in the gunfighter's baggage. Taking off his hat, he angled the barrel of his rifle down and put the dark snuff-colored hat on the muzzle. Then he slowly raised the weapon's barrel.

His ruse worked. An instant after he had raised the hat a shot cracked from the trees, followed quickly by another. Both slugs went wide. One whistled over the hat, the second kicked up a dusting of snow a yard ahead of it. Longarm had not taken his eyes off the pine forest. He saw the bright spurt of red muzzle-flash when each shot was fired and brought his rifle down quickly, letting his hat drop on the snow.

Shouldering the Winchester, he triggered off two quick shots that bracketed the place where he had seen the flashes, then put a third slug squarely into the spot where the muzzle-blast had showed. This time there was no answering fire.

By now Longarm's eyes were smarting from the cold and from looking into the brilliance of the sunrise. The rim of the rising sun was just clearing the tips of the pines and its rays striking the surface of the snow in front of Longarm's eyes were reflected by the crystallized flakes as brilliantly as though each of the billions of flakes was a tiny mirror. He reached for his hat and put it on, blinked several times, and shook his head to clear the teardrops that had formed at the rims of his eyelids. Then he turned his attention to the trees ahead.

He saw no movement, but he was not yet ready to expose himself. Instead of getting up and starting for the trees, Longarm belly-crawled the short distance necessary to reach his saddlebags. He opened the flap of the bag that held his spare ammunition and thumbed cartridges into his Winchester's loading port, then rebuckled the flap. Pushing the rifle muzzle under the flap of the bag he had just closed, Longarm angled the weapon upward. The saddlebags rose slowly, but brought no shot from the shadowed trees.

"Looks like he's took off, old son," Longarm muttered under his breath after he had held the saddlebags up for several moments. "But there's only one way to find out for sure, so the next move's up to you."

Keeping his eyes on the pine forest, Longarm rose to his feet, his rifle ready. There was no shot from the pines. Well aware that he had offered the Stovespit Kid an inviting target, Longarm could think of only one reason why the Kid had not taken advantage of his opportunity.

Nodding, he told himself silently, *More'n likely he found that rifle in the bunkhouse. It must not've had but four shells in the magazine, or he'd still be shooting. Which means you got him, old son, just as soon as you can catch up with him.*

Plodding through the snow to the spot where the shots had come from, Longarm saw the rifle lying across a heap of tattered blankets just inside the line of pine trees. Footprints in the snow leading down the slope to the west showed that the Stovespit Kid had started running again as soon as he had fired the last shot left in the rifle.

Well, that explains all of it, Longarm thought, stopping only long enough to glance at the evidence. *It ain't likely the Kid spotted me last night, but he'd've known I'd be sure to take after him. That bunkhouse is the only place he could've found that rifle and them blankets, so just as soon as he cut the chain he skedaddled off, figuring he'd bushwhack me this morning. Which he did, except he wasn't enough of a good shot to make his scheme work out.*

Following the Kid's tracks in the snow was no trick. Longarm spotted him less than ten minutes after he'd left the scene of the fugitive's failed ambush. The Kid was dodging through the pines a hundred yards ahead, taking long steps, unable to run fast in the deep snow. He had kept one of the blankets to wrap himself in, and its edges flapping in the light chilling wind made him look like some huge, ungainly bird trying vainly to get up the momentum to fly.

Longarm followed patiently, interested not only in keeping the Kid in sight, but in continuing to force him to move in the general direction of Truckee. He knew the Kid's advantage over him was limited to the lead he now held, and was counting on his own stamina to be great enough to outlast the Kid's.

Bit by bit, the Kid lost the race. Longarm could see the distance between them steadily shrinking, and he was sure the fugitive could notice it, too. They were less than fifty yards apart when the race ended suddenly. The Kid looked back, saw the gain Longarm had made, and while looking back dashed at full stride into the bole of one of the pine trees. Flailing his arms in a fruitless effort to regain his balance, the Kid fell backward into the soft snow.

Calling up some hidden reserve of energy, Longarm speeded up. He was within a dozen paces of the Kid, holding his rifle levelled, by the time the Kid had regained his feet. The Stovespit Kid took one look at the Winchester, raised his eyes to look at Longarm's set face, and raised his hands.

Longarm kept the rifle steady, and as he closed the gap between them he saw that the Kid had pulled the short length of chain left on each shackle up his legs and tied them below his knees with strips of cloth torn from one of the blankets he had taken from the bunkhouse.

For a moment, neither man spoke. They stared at one another, panting, both winded after the chase. It was the Stovespit Kid who broke the silence.

"You win this round, Marshal," he panted. His voice was strained and his ugly face twisted into a grimace which showed anger and disappointment. "But we're still a long way from Denver. I've slipped away from you twice now, and I'm betting I can do it again before we get there."

"You better copper that bet, because you'd sure lose it," Longarm told him. He was as winded as the Kid, but controlled his voice better. "I don't aim to give you a chance to try again. Turn around now, but keep your hands up."

Slowly, the Stovespit Kid obeyed. Longarm fished out his handcuffs, snapped a cuff over one of the Kid's wrists, pulled the manacled wrist down and behind his back, then snapped the manacle around his other wrist.

"I don't know if you've ever seen a man trying to run with his hands cuffed in back of him," he remarked casually. "But I've seen a lot of 'em try. The ones that don't fall down on their faces can't make very good time. If you feel like trying to take off again, you might just keep that in mind."

"Oh, I'll get away again," the Kid boasted. "But I'll be smart enough next time to pick a better time and place. Like I told you, Denver's still a long way off."

Longarm did not try to match the Stovespit Kid's boasting. He said quietly, "We'll eat the apple one bite at a time. The first thing we got to do is walk to Truckee, where we can catch a train."

"I need to rest a minute or two, Marshal," the Kid said, a plaintive note in his voice. "I haven't had a bite to eat since noon yesterday, and I'm weak as a kitten."

Longarm's voice held no pity as he replied, "You're about as weak as a full-grown catamount, the way you was running. There ain't no use trying to put me off, Kid."

"I don't suppose you've got anything to eat in your saddlebags?" the Kid pleaded.

"If I had, I'd've eaten breakfast myself, which I didn't. I'm just as hungry as you are, and the nearest place where we can get some grub is Truckee. So start walking."

"How far is Truckee?"

"Not more'n three or four miles, the way I figure it," Longarm replied. "Now get moving! I'll be walking right behind you, and I'll tell you right now I'm plumb out of patience with you. Step over the line one more time and I'll drop you in your tracks. Turn around without any more jawing, and let's get started."

Longarm was not greatly surprised when the Kid obeyed with unaccustomed meekness. He knew that his captive must be as hungry and tired as he was himself. They plodded through the snow, Longarm walking behind the Kid and keeping him moving in the direction he'd selected, a long, slanting course to the north and east that he was sure would take them back to the stagecoach road. The sun was high when they reached it, and Longarm's stomach kept reminding him how long it had been empty.

Once on the road, their progress was easier. It slanted in granite-walled zigzag cutbacks down the mountain flanks, and they could see Truckee long before they reached the road's final curve that brought them to the banks of the Truckee River and into the little town.

By now it was mid-afternoon, and Longarm's stomach was protesting its emptiness with almost constant cramping pangs. He and the Stovespit Kid had talked little during their long hike. In the thin air of the high Sierras, breath was too precious to waste. Both were tired, both hungry, and both still angry, Longarm at himself for letting the Kid escape in the first place, the Kid because he'd been recaptured after his getaway.

It was the Kid who broke the silence between them as they passed Truckee's first houses, dotted on a narrow mountain meadow west of the town. Looking over his shoulder at Longarm, he asked, "You going to feed me, now that we've finally got here? I don't mind telling you, my belly thinks my throat's been cut."

"If you think I'm any better off than you are, you're wrong," Longarm replied. "Sure, we'll eat. But if I ain't mistaken, that building right up ahead is a blacksmith shop. I aim to stop there long enough to get that chain put together again. I don't intend to give you another chance to wiggle away from me."

"Can't you let that wait until after we eat, Marshal?" the Kid asked. "Damn it, you must be as hungry as I am."

"Oh, I'm hungry, all right," Longarm admitted. "But I don't aim to eat before you're hobbled solid again. For one thing, that blacksmith shop might be the only one in this little one-horse town, and I don't cotton to the idea of going on in to eat and having to hike back out here again. I've done about all the walking I want to for right now."

"Well, I don't guess I've got much say about it," the Kid said glumly. "But you got to admit, I gave you a pretty good run for your money, considering what I had to work with."

"Not that it done you any good," Longarm pointed out.

"At least I had a chance to run, and to walk like a man instead of a damned hobbled horse," the Kid shot back. "Even if you did catch up with me, it was worth it."

"Make the most of it, then," Longarm told him. "You sure as hell ain't going to get a second chance. Now swing over to that blacksmith shop and let's get them leg irons fixed."

During the quarter of an hour the blacksmith took to put a new link on the chain, the Stovespit Kid paced restlessly back and forth across the back end of the shop. Longarm sat between the Kid and the door in the only chair the little blacksmith shop had. He kept his promise. Not once did he relax his vigilance while the Kid paced. When the job was finished and the Kid's ankles shackled again, Longarm motioned toward the door.

"All right," he said. "Now that my friend's at rest, we'll go on into town and get some grub. If we move sorta spry, we oughta finish supper in time to catch the eastbound Limited, and I don't mind telling you, we can't get to Denver too fast to suit me. I'll be right glad to turn you over to the jailer and not have to look at you anymore until you come to trial."

"All right, get over by the window, like you been doing," Longarm told the Stovespit Kid as they reached the last seat in the Western Pacific coach. "We ain't got a lot further to go, now. In about three more hours we'll be back in Denver, and I'll be be well rid of you. So will everybody else after the judge and the hangman do their jobs, which ain't going to take much time after the jury has its say."

Silently, the Kid obeyed. He settled into the seat and held

his right foot high to allow Longarm to unlock the shackle around his ankle. Longarm checked the legs of the seats and found that, unlike those on the Union Pacific, they were anchored solidly to both the seat and the floor. He passed the shackle around the leg and replaced the padlock, then settled into the aisle seat.

Neither man spoke while they were waiting for the train to move out of the Cheyenne depot. The Stovespit Kid stared out the window at the few people remaining on the station platform, as though he was taking a final look at a world he might never see again. Longarm hunched down in his seat, pushed his hat down over his eyes, and leaned back against the headrest, relaxing now that he had the Kid in close custody and was on the final leg of what had been anything but a routine trip.

At last the sharp blasts of the locomotive's whistle sounded and the car jolted as the engineer took up slack. The couplings whined, then grated as the coach began moving slowly ahead. The uninspiring vista of the railroad yards slid past the window. Then, as the locomotive gained speed, rows of small houses flashed past, then the town was left behind for the brown landscape, rolling winter-dry pastureland where patches of gray melting snow showed here and there against the dead grass.

"You asleep, Marshal?" the Kid asked hesitantly. When Longarm did not answer, he repeated the question, a bit louder this time.

"I was halfway asleep till you started jawing at me," Longarm replied at last. His voice was harsh as he pushed his hat back. "What's bothering you now?"

"Thinking about what you said just now. I don't guess it'd do any good for me swear I didn't shoot your friend in Denver, would it?"

"Not a damn bit. Ellie Benson seen you shoot her husband. She identified you from what she'd heard me and Jed Benson talking about when we seen that last Wanted circular for the job you pulled in Pueblo."

"Now, I ain't denying I held up the Pueblo post office," the Kid said after a moment.

150

"Not that it'd do you any good," Longarm told him, "when the clerk identified you so plain."

"Now, damn it, Marshal!" the Kid protested. "I wasn't going to hang around in Colorado after that job! I knew you federals would be after me for it right away. That's why I cut a shuck for California. I wasn't noplace near Denver when that federal marshal got shot!"

"That's about what I'd look for you to say," Longarm nodded. He was wide awake now, and still disgruntled from having his nap interrupted.

"I swear to God, Marshal, I didn't kill nobody!" the Kid protested. His ugly face was twisted into a protesting scowl, and there was a tremor of fear in his voice. "I was long gone from Denver when your friend got shot!"

His voice heavy with sarcasm, Longarm said, "And I guess you was asleep in bed in Denver and not anyplace near that logging camp up in the mountains when you tried to kill me."

"Stop making fun of me, Marshal!" the Kid said. "Can't you see I'm telling you the truth this time?"

Facing the Kid squarely, Longarm replied, "If I was ever certain that I'm looking at a liar, it's right this minute. I don't want to hear no more outa you, Kid."

"But, Marshal Long! Somebody's got to listen to me, somebody who'll believe me!"

"Oh, somebody's going to listen to you, all right," Longarm replied. "You'll have twelve jurors and a judge listening when you get in court charged with killing Jed Benson. Save your breath to try to get *them* to believe your yarns. Now, keep quiet! I want to get a little shuteye before this train gets to Denver."

Chapter 17

"We'll just sit tight until everybody else gets off. Then you won't have no chance to bust away and try to get lost in a crowd in the depot," Longarm told the Stovespit Kid as the train creaked to a halt in Denver.

"Don't worry about me trying to run again with these leg irons on," the Kid replied. "I'm not fool enough to make the same mistake twice. One time was plenty."

"Maybe. But just the same, I'll put the cuffs on your wrists first," Longarm said. "Hold out your hands."

With the handcuffs secured, Longarm unlocked one leg iron and freed the connecting chain from the seat-leg, then replaced the cuff on the Kid's leg.

"All right, let's move," he told the prisoner. "The crowd looks like it's thinned out enough, and likely Billy Vail or one of the deputies from the office will be inside the station to meet us. I sent Billy a telegram from Cheyenne telling him when I'd be delivering you."

All but a handful of the passengers from Cheyenne had left the depot by the time Longarm led the Stovespit Kid inside. Longarm looked around for Vail or one of his fellow deputies from the Denver office, but it was obvious at once that he was going to be alone in delivering his prisoner. He led the Kid outside and hailed a hack.

"Arapaho County jail," he told the driver as he settled to the seat beside the Kid. "And I'll want you to wait for me there till I get rid of this prisoner."

For the first few minutes after the hack pulled away from the depot the Kid was silent. Then he turned to Longarm and said, "You're going to be sorry about this some day, Marshal.

I was telling you the truth about not killing that deputy."

Longarm had heard much the same words from more killers than he could count, and the Kid's remark did not move him. He told the Kid, "I'll manage to get over being sorry, and I still don't believe it's in you to tell the truth."

"Be that as it may, you might ask yourself one queston, Marshal," the Kid said. His voice was very sober.

"What's that?"

"See if you can come up with any reason at all why I'd kill that friend of yours. As far as I know, I never set eyes on him anyplace, any time. If you can give me one reason why I'd shoot a man I don't know, one I haven't got any kind of a grudge against, I'd like to hear it."

"You wouldn't be the first outlaw that killed a lawman just because he was wearing a badge," Longarm reminded the Kid. His voice was as cold as the north wind in midwinter. "But you can't talk long enough or fast enough to make me change my mind."

During the rest of the ride the Kid remained silent. They reached the jail and Longarm led him inside. To his surprise, the head warden was waiting to greet him.

"Billy Vail dropped by in the afternoon to tell me you were bringing this fellow in tonight," he told Longarm. "Billy warned me about him being slick, so you won't have to go over it again. I thought a lot of Jed Benson, so I'm not going to give the man who killed him any chance to escape."

"I'll leave him with you and go on home, then," Longarm said. "I got a load of cinders to scrape off and all the dirt I collected chasing this son of a bitch over half of California, and about all I'm interested in is getting in a bathtub and having a good long soak."

Thoughts of the restful night ahead of him filled Longarm's mind as the hackney rattled over the spottily paved Denver streets to his rooming house on the wrong side of Cherry Creek. He paid the cabman and hauled his gear upstairs, then made a beeline for the bureau and the half-full bottle of Tom Moore. A healthy swallow of the pungent Maryland rye warmed his stomach, and he carried the bottle to the chair beside his bed.

Stripping to his longjohns, Longarm stretched out on the bed and lighted a cheroot. He was reaching for the bottle again when a rapping on the door stopped his hand in midair. Getting up grudgingly, he went to the door.

"Who is it?" he asked without opening it.

"Just me, Marshal Long," his landlady replied. "I've got a letter for you."

Longarm opened the door. The minute he saw the amber-colored envelope he knew who had sent the letter.

"Some kind of servant in a fancy uniform driving a shiny carriage brought this yesterday evening," the landlady went on. "Said it was real important. Told me he tried to deliver it at your office, but it was closed. I sure hope it ain't bad news."

"I don't imagine it is," Longarm replied, taking the letter. "And I thank you very much for taking care of it."

Before the landlady could reply, Longarm closed the door. He opened the letter as he went back to the bed and sat on the side of the bed to read it. The single sheet of amber paper bore only a few lines: *Longarm, my darling, I'm in town for three or four days. My business here will take up the daytime, but I'm saving the nights for you. Love, Julia.*

Longarm smiled as his eyes dwelled on the bold script and sprawling signature. He had nothing but pleasant memories of the few nights he had spent with Julia Burnside since rescuing her from an aggressive masher on a train bound for Denver. Julia, the daughter of a wealthy Eastern industrialist, stopped in the mile-high city only infrequently, but she always took pains to let Longarm know when she was in town.

Tilting the bottle of Tom Moore again, Longarm got his razor out of his saddlebags, took a towel from the rack fixed over the wash stand, picked up the splinter of soap from its dish, and started for the bathroom. He made quick work of a bath and shave and in less than a quarter of an hour he stepped out of the rooming house, enjoying the feeling of fresh clothes and the glow in his stomach from the swallow of Tom Moore he'd taken before leaving.

As he turned toward the Cherry Street bridge, Longarm

took out a cigar and stopped long enough to light it. He had almost reached the bridge when a buggy turned out of a side street and rolled toward him.

Ordinarily Longarm would have paid no attention to the buggy. They were common enough even in the run down area where his rooming house was located. But as it approached him the driver extinguished the carriage lamp attached to the curved dashboard.

Longarm's sixth sense was never idle. He frowned when he saw the running light go out, and though the interior of the buggy was shrouded in darkness his sharp eyes caught a shine of bright metal. Longarm was diving to the ground when the shining metal moved. He glimpsed a gloved hand holding a small steel revolver as he dived for the ground, and was whipping out his Colt before he hit the ground.

As Longarm rolled toward the darkness away from the walkway, a shot from the buggy broke the night's silence and a spurt of red muzzle-blast came from the nickled steel pistol followed by the splattering of a lead slug into the gravel.

Still rolling, Longarm answered with a shot from his Colt. The bullet thunked and wood splintered as it struck the buggy's body, and a second shot came from the driver's pistol.

Longarm was still moving, hidden now by the deep shadow away from the street. The buggy had rolled on past him and he heard the flat slapping of its reins on the horse's back. Rising to one knee, Longarm fired again, another unaimed shot that struck the street below the buggy.

By now the buggy was almost lost to sight in the darkness, though Longarm could still hear the grating of its wheels and the thunking hooves of the horse that pulled it. He got to his feet, his Colt dangling in his hand as he gazed into the darkness. The noise of wheels and hoofbeats was almost inaudible, and in the gloom he could only distinguish details for a few yards.

Seems like somebody's been waiting for you to get back home, old son, he considered as he took two fresh shells from the capacious pocket of his coat and reloaded. *Question is, who was it, and the likeliest answer's got to be that it was some crook you put away, trying to even the score. But chances are he'll try again, and maybe you'll get a better chance to see him, next time.*

Holstering his Colt, Longarm started walking up Colfax to the downtown section, where he knew he'd find a hack looking for a fare. He hailed the first one he saw, and settled down for the long ride to Sherman Avenue, still mulling over the effort to bushwhack him.

Even in the darkness, the Burnside mansion was imposing. Only two lighted windows, one on the ground floor, one from the second floor, shone from its dressed stone facade, but Julia Burnside herself opened the front door to Longarm's ring.

"Longarm!" she exclaimed when she saw him in the doorway.

Even in the semi-darkness of the entry, Julia's beauty stood out, the features of her oval face as perfect as a cameo, framed by her shoulder-length black hair, her generous breasts bulging under the thin fabric of her silk gown. Longarm waited for her to close the door and bent to kiss her upraised lips. They held the kiss until both were breathless, and when at last their lips parted Julia looked up at Longarm and smiled.

"I was wondering if you'd got my message," she said.

"You knew I wouldn't waste a minute getting here," he told her. "It's been too long since the last time you were here."

"I can't think of a nicer compliment," she said. "I was beginning to think you weren't coming."

"I just stepped off the train from California a couple of hours ago," Longarm said. "I got here as soon as I could."

"I suppose I'm lucky that you didn't meet some girl on the train, the way we met the first time," Julia said teasingly.

Longarm's first encounter with Julia had been on a train carrying them to Denver, when he'd saved her from the obnoxious overtures of a drunken drummer. Julia was the daughter of a wealthy New York industrialist who had built the mansion on Sherman Avenue when he'd acquired extensive interests in Western mining properties. Since she and Longarm first met, Julia had stopped over briefly in Denver several times, and had always let Longarm know when she was in town.

Now she said, "If you've been to California on a case, that means that you won't be leaving Denver right away." She took Longarm's hand and led him into the high-ceilinged room that adjoined the foyer. "I just might have to change my plans and stay a while longer than I'd intended to." She gestured toward the divan and went on, "If you want to, we can have a drink down here, or we can wait until we get up to my bedroom."

"I'd rather have you than a drink, but seeing as I can have both at the same time, I'd sooner go up to your room."

"I was sure you'd say that, or I never would have asked," Julia smiled, brushing a kiss across Longarm's lips.

Longarm put an arm around her waist as they crossed the big room to the stairway and half carried her up the carpeted steps. The door to Julia's bedroom stood ajar, a faint light spilling from it across the wide hall. When they entered the bedroom, Longarm paused and reached for the doorknob.

"Don't bother to close the door," Julia told him. "I didn't bring my maid this trip, and Evans wouldn't think of leaving his room over the stable unless I rang for him. We can be just as free as we want to be tonight."

"That suits me," Longarm said. He took off his hat and looked around for a place to put it.

"Throw it on a chair or the floor or anyplace but the bed," Julia told him. "We'll be using the bed—all night, I hope."

As Julia spoke she stepped up to Longarm's side and pressed her hand on his crotch. Her fingers explored and stroked until she could feel Longarm's shaft begin to swell. Longarm let his hat fall to the floor and shrugged out of his coat, then quickly unbuckled his gunbelt and dropped it on his coat as Julia kept up her soft caresses.

"Hurry, Longarm!" she urged. "I've been thinking of you ever since the train left Kansas City!"

"That's a long time to wait," he said. "But I'm hurrying fast as I can."

Julia's breathing was becoming ragged now, and her breasts rose and fell as the words gusted from her lips. She waited until Longarm had levered out of his boots and while he was dropping his trousers to the floor she began pulling his underwear down his chest and to his thighs.

157

"Take me to bed!" she urged, pulling at the sash of her negligee and letting it slither to the floor. Her body was trembling, her hips rotating.

Lifting her bodily, Longarm stepped to the bed. Julia was still quivering when he lowered her to the satin sheets. Longarm went into her swiftly, burying his shaft full-length with one quick lunge, and she shrieked with joy when he began stroking.

He drove like a triphammer for only a few minutes before she shrieked again as she began an orgasm that set her to twisting and bouncing while Longarm continued to stroke until her throbbing cries grew softer and trailed away into silence.

Longarm did not let up. He slowed the pace of his thrusts, going into her deeply and almost gently until she started to respond again. Her soft body quivering, Julia began bouncing her hips upward as though to take Longarm's deep penetrations even more completely, and he matched her increasingly frenzied rhythm.

When Julia's entire body began shaking she locked her legs around Longarm's hips and pulled him into her when he thrust down. Long moments passed, the room quiet now except for the sounds of their hoarse breathing, then Julia's quivering grew into another wild frenzy. Longarm speeded up, moving to his own peak now.

When Julia's cry of satisfaction filled the room, he let himself go and jetted. Julia moaned deep in her throat while she shook and tossed, and finally with a deep sigh relaxed completely. Only then did Longarm let his body go slack and rest quietly on Julia's warm, quivering flesh.

Julia broke the silence at last. She said, "I don't know how you manage to do it, Longarm, but you're still as big and hard as ever. Maybe that's what brings me back to you time after time. You know that I meet other men, travelling the way I do, but none of them satisfies me the way you do."

"We do hit it off," Longarm agreed. "And you know how I feel about you."

"I think I do." Julia smiled up at him. "But is it too soon for you to give me another demonstration?"

"Not a bit. I was thinking the same thing myself."

"You must be tired, though," she said. "Let me get on top this time. Can you stay all night?"

"I wouldn't want to stay anyplace else but where I am right now," he assured her. "Take your time, Julia. There ain't no need to hurry. We got all the rest of the night ahead of us."

Chapter 18

"Swing over and take Arapaho Street the rest of the way downtown, Evans," Longarm told the Burnside coachman as the carriage approached the business district. "That's where most of the livery stables are. I don't know which one I'm looking for, so it's liable to take a while to find it. I'll just get out at the first one we come to and and walk along asking questions, then go on and walk the rest of the way to my office."

Acknowledging Longarm's instructions with a nod, the coachman turned the carriage into Arapaho. Longarm settled back on the velour-upholstered seat and relaxed with a contented smile as he recalled the night just past and anticipated the two nights yet to come before Julia resumed her trip west.

"I'm going to claim every minute of the time you have free until I leave," she had told him after he had reluctantly agreed to let her have the coachman take him to the federal building. "We don't have much, but if it doesn't interfere with your plans—"

"Now, you know better'n that, Julia," he'd broken in. "I still got to close this case I been on, and I got a little bit of digging to do on another one, but the only plan I got is just the same as yours. You don't get to Denver all that often."

Longarm's pleasant thoughts were broken when the coachman pulled up in front of a livery stable. He got out of the carriage before Evans could step down from his high seat at the front. Longarm gestured for the coachman to go on, then stepped into the livery stable.

"I guess you rent buggies and other kind of traps," he said to the overall-clad man who was coming slowly to meet him.

"Sure do, mister. Are you looking to rent a buggy?"

160

"Not right now. Fact is, I'm trying to find one that's got a fresh bullet hole or two in it." Taking out his wallet, Longarm opened it to show his badge. "I ain't just a busybody. This is official business."

"Well, you won't find no bullet holes in the two buggies I got," the liveryman said. "Look for yourself, if you want to."

"Your word's good," Longarm told him. "But if you hear about any of the other liveries that's had a buggy shot up, I'd take it kindly if you'd send word to me at the federal building. My name's Long. If I ain't around, just leave word."

"Be glad to oblige you," the liveryman nodded. "But if any of the other liveries had a buggy shot up, I ain't heard about it yet."

Making his way down the street, Longarm stopped at three more livery stables before hitting pay dirt.

"I sure as hell did, Marshal!" the stable owner replied indignantly to Longarm's questioning. "The damn buggy wasn't just shot up, either. I guess whatever happened to start somebody shooting must've spooked whoever rented it."

"Oh? How's that?"

"Why, they just got out of the damn rig and walked away. Didn't even take the trouble to hitch my horse to a lamppost or something. I didn't get the rig back until just a little while ago, when the fellow from one of the liveries down the street happened to see the horse plodding along loose and brought the buggy back to me."

"You remember what the fellow who rented the rig looked like?"

"I don't, because I wasn't around. My night man was on when the rig was rented, and he took off for Shambala soon as I relieved him this morning. He's visiting relations, and won't be back for two or three days."

"I guess you got the name of whoever rented it, though?"

The livery man frowned. "Sure. I ain't fool enough to rent one of my rigs unless I get the name of whoever takes it out. But I figure they must've been up to some kinda underhanded work, because the first thing I did was to go looking for the renter."

"Mind telling me who it was?"

"Not a bit. The rent-out book's signed by somebody that called theirself Adams. No first name. Just J. Adams. And there's not even a house at the address they put down."

"Well, that answers some questions," Longarm said. "But the answers ain't the kind I'm looking for. Mind if I take a look at that buggy, and then at your ledger?"

"Not a bit. If it's all the same to you, I'll show you the ledger before we go out back. It's right over there on my desk."

Longarm stepped over to the desk with the liveryman and bent over the ruled page to which the ledger was opened. The name on the line where the man placed his finger was a neatly printed "J. Adams," followed by an address on Pecos Street.

"That's a pretty far way out from town," the livery owner said. "But I was mad enough after I saw that buggy to close up and go looking for this Adams fellow. There's not many houses on Pecos yet, and there wasn't anything but a vacant lot at that address. I asked at the house nearest to it, and there never has been a house there, or nobody by the name of Adams in the neighborhood."

"I sorta had a hunch I'd run into something of this kind," Longarm told him. "Now I'll take a quick look at the buggy, if you don't object."

"Look all you want to, Marshal. If you're after whoever hired that buggy, I'd like nothing better'n to see 'em caught."

Longarm's examination of the buggy was as fruitless as his examination of the ledge had been. The buggy had a fresh scar on the spokes of one of its back wheels and a bullet hole in the seat-back, with a ripped spot in the upholstery where another bullet had entered and emerged, but that was all.

Shaking his head, Longarm said, "Looks to me like it's a dead-end road until your night man gets back. And I got an idea it's not going to do me much good to talk to him."

"You're looking for this Adams fellow, too, I take it?"

"I sure am. You see, I'm the one that put the bullet in your buggy. Whoever had it out last night took a couple of potshots at me while I was walking up Cherry Street. I shot back, a-course, but it was just a couple of snap shots in the dark."

"Well, I'll be damned!" the liveryman gasped. "No wonder

you're so interested! Well, I'll tell you, Marshal Long, if you find that fellow, I'd like to know about it. He left a five-dollar deposit on the rig, and that'll cover the rent, but it's going to cost more'n that to fix up my buggy."

"When I catch up with him, I'll sure let you know," Longarm promised. "Matter of fact, when he comes to trial, you and your night man both will likely be called as witnesses."

"You talk like you got an idea who this Adams fellow is," the liveryman frowned.

Longarm shook his head. "Not yet. But in the kind of job I got, when somebody tries to gun me down, I take a real personal interest in finding out who it was. Meantime, I thank you for your help. Now, I got to be getting along. My chief is likely going to be upset, because I'm late already."

Chief Marshal Billy Vail was indeed upset when Longarm walked into the office in the federal building.

"Where the hell have you been since that train pulled in last night?" he asked. "Out on the town, I guess, instead of reporting in here at eight o'clock."

"Not on your life, Billy," Longarm shot back. "I was on the job at eight, but before reporting in I stopped at a few places trying to get a line on the no-good son of a bitch that tried to stop my clock last night."

"Are you telling me somebody tried to kill you?"

"They sure as hell did. And before you go off half-cocked again, it wasn't over a poker game or a woman. At least, not as far as I know."

"When did all this happen?" Vail frowned, motioning for Longarm to sit down.

Longarm took his time, pulling his favorite chair up to the corner of the marshal's desk and lighting a cheroot before asking, "How do you want the story, Billy? Just when I was shot at, or what I done since I got to town?"

"I'll get your report later. Tell me what this shooting last night was all about."

"Your guess is as good as mine," Longarm said. "All I know is that I was walking up Cherry Street from my rooming house about ten o'clock and seen a buggy heading toward me.

Whoever was in it took two shots at me. Lucky they was using a fancy whore's pistol, one of them shiny nickel-plated popguns, so I seen it flashing before they could take good aim."

"Which gave you time to draw and—" Vail stopped and cocked his head as he looked at Longarm through narrowed eyes. "Wait a minute! You had time to get off a shot or two, didn't you?"

"Oh, sure. The thing about it is, I'd hit the ground when I seen the gun. I hadn't quit rolling when I got off my shots, so all I hit was the buggy."

"And whoever was in the buggy got away," Vail said. "Well, it's not like you to miss, Long, but I suppose you got a good look at whoever was behind the gun?"

"I didn't even get a good look at the damn gun! I was lucky to put a couple of slugs in the back of the buggy while it was getting away. It was dark as pitch. They ain't put up none of them fancy new lights on that part of the street yet. But the pistol sounded like it was a .36 or maybe even a .32. I was more interested in saving my hide than I was in the artillery."

"I sure can't blame you," Vail agreed. "But that was last night. What's it got to do with you being late this morning?"

"Let me ask you a question for a change, Billy," Longarm said, leaning forward in his chair. "Did you ever see something when you was in a tight spot, and not have it come to you till later that you seen it?"

Vail frowned thoughtfully, taking his time to answer, then replied slowly, "I think I see what you mean, and the answer's yes. When you're in a showdown and somebody's shooting at you, later on you'll remember something you saw but didn't notice at the time. Everybody does that now and then. Hell, we talk to witnesses all the time who've had it happen to them."

Nodding, Longarm went on, "Well, it wasn't until real late last night that I remembered what I'd seen on that buggy. It was one of them little number plates the city makes liveries put on the rigs they rent out. And that's why I'm so late checking in this morning. For the last hour or more I been going along Arapaho, trying to find that buggy."

"Did you find it?"

"Oh, sure, even if it did take some time. I know it's the same buggy, because one of my slugs went through the back of the seat and the other one nicked a spoke. The trouble is that the man who rented it out last night wasn't there for me to ask what the fellow that rented it looked like."

"You'll go back later today and talk to him, then," Vail said.

Longarm shook his head. "Not today, Billy. The fellow's gone off for a visit to his kinfolk. He won't be back for two or three days."

"I'll have one of the other men take care of it, then," Vail said. His voice was very casual.

Longarm almost jumped out of his chair as the implication registered. Narrowing his eyes, he asked, "You ain't planning to send me out on another case right away, are you, Billy? I ain't had time to catch my breath since I been back."

"It's not a new case," Vail said. "You haven't closed out the one you've been on, yet."

"You're holding something back on me, Billy. There's too many times when I've seen you look like you're looking now. I know it when you've got something up your sleeve. Now, I brought the Stovespit Kid back here and delivered him to the county jail. It's up to the lawyers from here on in. Far as I can see, the case is finished, all right."

"You haven't filed a report yet," Vail pointed out. "It's just as well you haven't, because something new came up while you were gone."

"You better tell me what it is, Billy," Longarm said resignedly. "I oughta be used to your ways by now, but I sure can't figure out what you're talking about."

"We've been wrong about the Stovespit Kid," Vail replied. "Right from the beginning. He didn't kill Jed Benson. He was in jail in some little jerkwater town up in the Idaho Panhandle when Jed was murdered."

When Longarm heard the chief marshal's unexpected statement, his jaw dropped so fast that his cigar fell from his mouth. He caught the cheroot and juggled it from one hand to the other, trying to avoid getting burned by its coal. When he'd finally gotten hold of the cigar he asked, "Now what in hell do you mean, Billy?"

"Just exactly what I said," Vail replied. "I suppose you remember that I sent out Wanted fliers on the Kid?"

"Sure. That's why the police department in Oakland wired us when they arrested him."

"Well, it turns out that they weren't the only ones who sent us an answer. A day or so after I got your wire that you were leaving Oakland with the Kid, I got a letter from the town marshal in someplace called Kamiah. That's up in the Idaho Panhandle. It must be a hard place to get to, because he didn't get the flier for a couple of weeks after they went out."

"And he say he was holding the Stovespit Kid in jail up there when Jed was shot?"

Vail nodded. "That's about the size of it. He gave me the dates when he locked up the Kid and when the Kid escaped—"

"He broke out of jail up in Idaho, too?" Longarm asked, incredulous.

"What would you expect?" Vail countered. "But that's not what's important. The Kid was in jail in Kamiah the very day that Jed got killed. There wasn't any way he could've been up there and here in Denver at the same time."

"You're sure this marshal in Idaho knows what he's talking about, Billy?"

"He wouldn't have any reason to lie," Vail pointed out. "I wired him for all the details, and he sent them to me. In fact, I got his letter just about the time you were leaving California to bring the Kid back here."

"You could've sent me a wire about all this, Billy." Longarm said sadly. "It sure would've saved me a mess of time and trouble."

"I did. I sent you a wire in care of the Oakland police, but Chief Edwards wired back that the Stovespit Kid had escaped and you'd started out to find him."

"Which I did," Longarm nodded. "And I don't guess there was much of a way you could've run me down with a wire, because I chased the Kid over half of California before I caught up with him." Longarm's cigar was now a stub clenched between his teeth. He dropped the chewed-up butt into Vail's spittoon and lighted another one before asking, "Well, what in hell are we going to do with the Kid now?"

"Don't worry," Vail replied. "It's not going to be hard to get rid of him. I've got a dozen Wanted calls on him since we sent out that flier saying we were after him. All you'll have to do is deliver him to whoever I decide to pass him on to."

"Oh, now hold up right there, Billy!" Longarm protested. "I looked at his ugly face all the way back here from California! It seems to me like whoever wants him bad enough oughta be willing to come get him!"

"How far do you think they'd get before he got away again?"

Longarm did not reply at once. He took a deep draw on his cigar and exhaled a cloud of blue smoke before he finally said, "I see what you're driving at, Billy. I wouldn't guarantee they'd get him outa the Denver city limits. He's the slipperiest man I ever ran into."

"Just count on the Kid being your job, then," Vail said. "But don't start making any travel plans yet."

"Maybe you better tell me what you're driving at," Longarm frowned. "A minute ago, you sounded like you was going to get rid of the Kid in the next day or so."

"That was my idea until you told me about somebody trying to gun you down last night. I've been doing a little bit of thinking while we were talking. As far as I'm concerned, we'll just hang onto the Stovespit Kid for a little while."

"If the jailers are able to," Longarm put in quickly.

"I'll have a talk with the warden about that," Vail promised. "But you've got two more jobs to take on before we ship out the Stovespit Kid."

"Well, I got to admit I'd like to run down whoever it was tried to gun me down last night," Longarm said.

"That's one of them, of course," the chief marshal said. "But the other case you'll be taking on is just as important."

"What've you got in mind now?"

"If the Stovespit Kid didn't shoot Jed Benson, somebody else did," Vail said slowly. "And since you were about the best friend Jed had, I'm going to put you on the job of finding out who that somebody else was."

Chapter 19

"That's a job you know I can't say no to, Billy."

"It's a job I ought to take on myself," Vail said, then nodded toward the papers stacked in untidy heaps on his desk. "But if I did, I'd get behind in this damned mess. It's a job that's got to be done, though, and the sooner the better. Before we let that slippery little crook get out of our hands, we've got to find out a lot more than we know now."

"I didn't have much luck getting anything at all out of the Stovespit Kid on the way back here," Longarm reminded the chief marshal. "But if he didn't gun Jed down, it could've been some other crook that was carrying a grudge."

"Of course," Vail agreed. "Remember that before Jed put on his marshal's badge, he was with the Denver police department. You might have to dig in the case file he left there."

"That's a long time back, Billy." Longarm frowned. "But it could've been somebody Jed had brought in a long time back. You know how crooks sit and think when they're in the pen for a stretch, plotting to settle up some old score. Trouble is, I don't know all that much about the cases Jed had worked."

"You will before you're through," Vail promised. "I'll have the clerk get out his case file. You can start there. Going through his records might give you some ideas about somebody he brought in who'd have reason to carry a grudge."

"You know how I hate to paw through papers, Billy," Longarm sighed. "If it was anybody but Jed . . ." He stopped, shook his head, and went on, "I'll get on it first thing tomorrow."

"What's wrong with today?" Vail asked, then went on pointedly, "Since you've already had half the morning off."

"I told you I was trying to find out who was sniping at me last night," Longarm protested.

Vail sat thoughtfully for a moment, then nodded. "All right," he said. "Do it your own way. If I know you, you'll do things your own way anyhow, regardless of what I tell you. Go ahead. Just let me see some results real soon."

"I hated to hear that clock chime midnight," Julie Burnside said.

She was sitting naked on the side of the bed, looking down at Longarm, who was stretched out in its center. He was as naked as Julia. She leaned down, propped herself on an elbow, took his flaccid shaft in her hand, and began squeezing and releasing it in a slow, pulsing caress.

"Well, I didn't like it any better'n you did," he told her. He did not move. He was already beginning to feel his groin growing taut in response to her caresses. "It was you that said we'd have to get ready to leave a little after twelve. But if you keep on feeling me that way, we ain't going anyplace for a while."

"I know," she said. "But at this time of night it's almost sinful to have to get out of a warm bed and dress and get on a train. We should've skipped having supper."

"We didn't," he reminded her. "And I sure wouldn't want to be blamed for getting your daddy mad at you because you missed your train to California."

"You're right, of course," Julia nodded. Releasing him reluctantly, she stood up and crossed the room to the closet, where her travelling clothes were hanging inside the open door.

"It ain't that I want to see you go," Longarm said. He rolled off the bed and reached for his longjohns, which lay in a crumpled heap on a chair beside the bed. "And I sure am going to miss you. But maybe you can stay more than a day or two the next time you come to Denver."

"I'd stay longer this time, if I could," she told him. "But if I don't meet Father on that train, I know the kind of fuss he'd raise when I did get to San Francisco."

They finished dressing in silence, and had little to say in

the carriage as they rode to the station. When the coachman pulled up at the depot, Julia said, "You'd better wait in the carriage, Longarm. As soon as Evans takes my luggage to the baggage room, he'll come back and drive you home."

"Now, I don't expect him to do that," Longarm protested. "I can get a hackney cab and —"

"I've already told Evans what to do," Julia broke in. "And don't come to the platform with me. Father will be watching for me from a window, and he'll plague me with questions the rest of the trip. He thinks it's a scandal that I'm not married yet, but I enjoy my life just the way it is. Kiss me goodbye, now, and be here when I get back on my next trip."

"That's one thing you can count on for sure," Longarm promised as he bent to find her lips with his.

They clung together until the whistle of the train pulling into the depot broke the night's stillness. Julia drew back, whispered a final goodbye, and hurried to the door of the depot without looking back.

Evans appeared out of nowhere to say, "Miss Julia has given me my instructions, Marshal Long. I'll take you to your home at once."

Closing the carriage door, the coachman mounted to his seat and a moment later the carriage rolled away from the depot. Longarm lighted a cheroot and leaned back, his mind turning to the case he had thought was closed. In spite of his exertions in bed with Julia earlier in the evening, he was not at all sleepy, and as he mulled over the job that was waiting for him, the thought of sleep was pushed farther into the background. The carriage was turning into Champa Street now, and Longarm reached a quick decision. Leaning forward, he opened the flap behind Evans's seat.

"I changed my mind about going home," Longarm told the coachman. "Drop me off at the federal building instead."

As Longarm had expected, lights were still shining through several windows of the imposing stone structure. He went up the alley to the back door, and after he'd pounded on its metal-sheathed surface for several minutes the night custodian opened the door.

"Marshal Long." The man frowned. "Something really bad

170

must've happened to bring you here this late at night."

"Not this time," Longarm said. "I just got to go up to the office and wind up a job I didn't have time to finish when I knocked off today. I don't guess you'd mind opening it up for me, would you?"

"Not a bit. The cleaning women have already finished on your floor, so I'll just take my lantern and go along to open the door for you."

"I'd appreciate it," Longarm told him.

He followed the custodian up the narrow back stairs, his boot heels thudding on the wooden steps. The custodian opened the office with his passkey and held his lantern high while Longarm lighted a lamp, then said, "When you finish, be sure you pull the door shut good. Them new patent locks we just put on save me a lot of work, letting folks go out without me having to follow them around with my keys."

"Thanks," Longarm said. "I don't know how long it'll take me to get caught up, but I aim to finish before I quit."

Wearily, Longarm pulled the sheafs of loose papers into a stack and put them back into their manila file folder. He rubbed his eyes, which were smarting from the unaccustomed strain of reading for several hours by lamplight, a job that had been complicated by trying to decipher Jed Benson's handwriting.

You ain't got much to be proud of about your own hen-tracks, old son, he told himself. *But up alongside these scratches poor old Jed made, you write as good as a schoolmarm.*

For all the painstaking care Longarm had given the job he'd made absolutely no progress. The case reports he had just finished reading covered Jed Benson's entire career as a deputy United States marshal, and none of them had contained any helpful clues or suggested a line of further inquiry.

But there's something real wrong someplace, Longarm's thoughts ran on. *Unless some reports is missing outa this file, Jed never did have a case that the Stovespit Kid was mixed up in. Course, there'd likely be times when Jed never filed a report, or maybe Henry put some of Jed's papers in the wrong place. Outside of that happening, there ain't a single damned report in this file that'd show Jed ever even seen the Kid. So why in the hell did Ellie get the idea it was him that shot Jed?*

That's a question you're going to have to ask her, his thoughts ran on. *She mentioned Jed had told her about the Stovespit Kid; that's how she was able to identify him for Billy Vail. She said Jed had made a case against him and it was from what Jed told her that she could recognize the Kid when he done the shooting. But she didn't say what kind of case Jed made.*

Then there's the Kid himself. He swore all the time coming back from California that he didn't gun Jed down.

A key grating in the lock of the office door interrupted Longarm's train of thought. He glanced up just as the door swung open and the clerk, Henry, came in.

"Marshal Long!" he exclaimed. "I didn't expect to see you on the job at this early hour of the morning!"

"Just because I don't happen to be tied down to a desk don't mean I ain't working," Longarm said. "But I'm glad you're here. I got a few questions I need to ask you about Jed Benson's case file. Are you sure you got all his cases in here?"

"Of ourse I'm sure!" the clerk answered indignantly. "Part of my job is to see that there's a complete record of all the deputies' cases in their files."

"Don't you reckon Jed might've done like I do now and then, and forget to make out a report, or get one in late? Or don't you figure you could've maybe put one or two of his reports in the wrong file?"

"Why, I can't be positive of something like that," Henry frowned. "Now, I'm sure that your own file isn't at all complete, Marshal Long. But not all the other deputies are as lax as you are in handing me their reports."

"I'll tell you what I'm going to ask you to do, then," Longarm went on. "You go over all the case files you got with a fine-tooth comb, and see if you can turn up something."

"'Something' covers a lot of ground, Marshal Long. Just exactly what do you expect me to look for?"

"Anything about the Stovespit Kid. His real name's Chauncey Mahoney, in case you don't already know. It don't necessarily have to be connected up with Jed. Any file you find that's got the Kid's name or Jed's in it, pull it out and have it waiting for me when I get back."

"Now, that's going to be a great deal of work," the clerk objected. "I'm not sure I can get to it—"

"Then maybe you better *make* sure," Longarm broke in. "I tell you what. When Billy Vail comes in, you pass on the word to him that I'm heading over to the Denver police headquarters to see what kind of files they got that might help us. Then you ask him if he wants you to go through our files, like I just told you to. And if he tells you any different from what I did, you pass the word to me when I get back, and I'll ask him myself."

When Longarm stepped out into the brisk morning air, his stomach began reminding him that he was an hour overdue for breakfast. Stopping at the first restaurant he came to, he put away a platter of ham and eggs and fried potatoes, washed down with two cups of steaming black coffee. His stomach quieted, he walked on to Denver police headquarters.

Big Ed McGruder, Denver's chief of police, squinted at Longarm across his desk. "I sure do wish I could help you, Long," he said. "I've got no sympathy for anybody that shoots a lawman, whether he's one of my officers or not. But the fact is, we don't keep our files the way you federal men do."

"I can't say I blame you for that," Longarm said. "I just finished going through some of ours, and there's more damn sheets of paper in 'em than a man can count. But you're bound to have some kind of records."

"Oh, we've got records, all right," McGruder replied. "A lot more than we can handle. That's why we go through them every five years and clean house. All the little petty crimes and closed case files go into a bonfire. And it was just last week that we burned the ones that'd have Jed Benson's cases. Jed's been with your outfit something like seven years now."

"I guess it has been that long," Longarm nodded. "It seems to me the longer I live, the shorter a year lasts."

"Now, I don't know who there'd be on the force today that could tell what you're trying to find out," the police chief went on. "But I'll be glad to put it on the roll-call list. The sergeants might turn up one of the officers who'd know something about the time when Jed first arrested that Stovespit Kid."

"I'd be real obliged if you'd do that," Longarm said. "I'm on my way out now to talk to Ellie and see what she remembers about Jed arresting the Kid. But anything more that you can dig up sure might help."

When Ellie opened the door and saw Longarm, she showed plainly that she was embarrassed.

"I hope you're not still made at me," she said. "I guess I made a fool out of myself, doing what I did, trying to take the law into my own hands."

"I wasn't all that mad at you, Ellie," Longarm replied. "I can understand how you felt. But the law's the law, and I swore I'd uphold it when I put on my badge. What you had your mind set on doing was to break the law, and I didn't have no choice but to stop you."

"Well, come in," Ellie said. "I guess you've got some reason for coming to see me. If it was just a friendly call, you'd more likely have come after supper than this time of day."

"It's business, all right," Longarm told her, following her into the living room of the bungalow. Ellie motioned to a chair, and as Longarm settled into it she sat down on the sofa.

"About what happened to Jed?"

"More or less," Longarm nodded. "It's something you told me about a while back, about when you was going looking for Jed the day he got killed."

Ellie sat silent for several moments, then said in a small, tight voice, "I've been trying to forget all about that, Longarm. Do I have to remember it all over again now?"

"I'm afraid you do," he answered. "But I ain't going to push you, Ellie. You take all the time you need to think before you answer what I've got to ask you, and I'll help you all I can if you need help."

Again Ellie was silent for a moment before replying. She sighed, then nodded and told Longarm, "Well, if I must, I guess I can stand it. What is it you want to know?"

"When me and Billy Vail was talking to you right after Jed got shot, you said you knew who the Stovespit Kid was from what Jed had told you about him," Longarm said. "You remember that, I guess?"

"How could I ever forget it?" Ellie asked, her eyes turned toward the floor. "It was right after he'd gunned Jed down."

"Jed had described the Kid for you?"

"Oh, yes. When he'd handled a case a long time ago."

"How long ago, Ellie?"

"Three or four years, I suppose. Maybe longer."

"You and Jed had been married before Jed handled the case, then?" Longarm frowned. When Ellie nodded, he went on, "How long had you been married, then, when that case came up?"

"Why, I don't remember all that much about it, Longarm," Ellie frowned. "And I don't remember what it was Jed had told me that made me recognize the Stovespit Kid when he was getting away after he'd shot Jed."

"Try to remember," Longarm urged. "It's important, Ellie. Could that case Jed had have been while he was still on the Denver police force?"

"I—I guess it could've been," she nodded.

"But you can't be sure?"

Ellie shook her head, then exclaimed unhappily, "You've got me all confused now, Longarm! I can't seem to think right! Please, don't ask me any more questions!"

"I've got to find out, Ellie," Longarm told her. "You see, Billy Vail's just got a letter from a town marshal up in the Idaho Panhandle. He says the Stovespit Kid was in jail there at the time Jed was shot."

Chapter 20

For a moment Ellie sat silent, her mouth open, staring at Longarm. Then she gasped, "That's impossible! I saw him shoot Jed, just like I said I did!"

"Maybe you better tell me again what you saw that night," Longarm suggested.

"Do I really have to?" Ellie's voice was pleading.

"I don't see no way around it. Billy Vail says he can't figure out any reason why that man up in Idaho would be lying, but just the same, I aim to take the Kid up to the office where me and Billy can question him some more. It looks now like you just made a mistake when you identified him."

"But I can't be mistaken!" Ellie insisted. "I know I'm right, Longarm!"

"If it was up to me—" Longarm began.

Ellie interrupted him. "Please! Don't let Billy send the man that murdered Jed off to someplace where he can't be made to pay for it!"

"You know it ain't up to me, Ellie," Longarm told her. "I can't tell Billy what to do, even if I might not cotton much to what he says. He's the chief marshal, not me."

"Then will you do me a favor?" Ellie asked. Her voice was calmer now.

"If I can, sure."

"Don't ask me any more questions right now, Longarm. I'm just too confused and upset to answer them."

"Putting it off ain't going to change anything," he pointed out. "Sooner or later—"

"I know," she broke in. "But couldn't you give me a little time to think back over what happened that night Jed was shot, and see if I can remember anything else?"

"I don't see no reason why I can't come back out later on," Longarm said slowly. "I got a few more things to do. I aim to get the Kid outa the county jail and haul him over to the office where Billy and me can both question him. That's going to take a while. And on my way back to town, I figure it'd be a good idea for me to stop by that saloon where you went to get Jed and see if the barkeep's remembered anything more."

"That's going to take up most of the morning," Ellie said. Her voice and manner were calmer now. "Come back right after noon, then, Longarm. I'll feel better after I've had a chance to let my nerves settle down."

"Sure," Longarm nodded. "Now, you just take things easy, Ellie. Billy Vail ain't about to close this case until he's got all the answers. I'll be back after noon, then, and see if you've thought about something you missed telling us before."

"Oh, sure, I haven't forgot anything that happened that evening," the barkeep replied in response to Longarm's question. "Jed Benson was one of our regulars."

"I was Jed's friend a long time," Longarm said. "And he never was what I'd call a two-fisted drinker."

"Well, that's right," the barkeep agreed. "He'd stop in most days for a shot on his way home to supper, but one or two was always about his limit. You ought to know that, you were in here with him once in a while." Indicating the bottle on the bar in front of Longarm, the man added, "I remember you, because we don't get many customers who ask for Maryland rye."

Nodding, Longarm went on, "That day he got killed, do you recall a real ugly fellow that might've been in here when Jed come in?"

"A lot of our customers ain't what you'd call handsome, Marshal. They're mostly working men that live in the neighborhood. I can't really remember seeing any of them that was uglier than usual, now that you've started me thinking back on it."

"Ellie Benson tells me she came down here looking for Jed the day he was killed," Longarm went on. "Did she do that very often?"

After a moment's thought, the barkeep shook his head. "If she was here, I didn't see her. Not that it's likely I would, though. Ladies don't come in here, Marshal. Now and again one of them will poke her head through the batwings, looking for her husband, but that's as close as they get to coming inside."

"I guess that's what Ellie would do, when she'd come here looking for Jed?"

"Now that you've started me thinking about it, I don't recall even seeing her do that more than two or three times," the barkeep frowned.

"You didn't see the shooting, I understand," Longarm went on. "But you do recall Jed being here just before it happened?"

"I guess I do," the man said slowly. "That's our busy time of day, you know; men going home from work. They step up for a quick one and go on. They don't usually stay around long."

"Well, I thank you for your help," Longarm said. He tossed off the rest of his drink. "If you should think about anything else that happened that evening, I'd take it kindly if you'd come down to the federal building and tell me about it."

Walking on toward the center of town, Longarm crossed Larimer and turned toward the county jail. He reached the cut stone building, which looked small now beside the bulk of the warehouses that for the past several years had been pushing rapidly toward it along the spur of the Santa Fe which curved through that section of Denver. The noon hour was near and the brick-paved streets were deserted as Longarm went into the jail.

"I got to take that man you're holding for us down to the office," he told the turnkey. "Bill Vail wants to ask him some more questions before we send him on. So do I, as far as that goes."

"Just sign him out and I'll go get him," the turnkey nodded. "I'll be glad to get rid of him, even for a little while. He keeps acting like this place is a damned hotel, and I'm tired of listening to him."

"I thought I'd seen the last of you, Marshal," the Stovespit Kid greeted Longarm jauntily. "But I hope you've come to let me out of here. I guess you've found out by now that I was telling you the truth about not shooting that deputy."

"We'll talk about that later," Longarm said curtly. He had no intention of telling the Kid anything until they were in Billy Vail's office with Vail himself. He took out his handcuffs and shackled his prisoner's wrists, then went on, "We're going to take a little walk, now. But don't try any of your tricks on me, because I'd still just as soon shoot you as look at you."

"Mind telling me where we're going?" the Stovespit Kid asked as Longarm led him down the wide hall toward the door. "Not that it makes a lot of difference, I guess. I'm just curious."

"You'll find out soon enough," Longarm replied. "And do me a favor. Just keep that big mouth of yours from wagging so much. I had all of your palaver I want on the way back here from California. You'll have plenty of time to chatter later on."

Keeping a firm hold on the Stovespit Kid's arm, Longarm pulled the door open and maneuvered him through the doorway into the building's narrow arched entryway. A flight of wide stone steps led down to the sidewalk. The Kid started down the steps ahead of Longarm, who had to lean forward and stretch to avoid losing his grip on his prisoner's arm.

A shot cracked and a bullet hit the edge of the entry. The lead pellet ricocheted and thudded into the Stovespit Kid. He lurched forward, pulling Longarm off-balance.

Longarm was still holding the Kid's arm with his right hand. Before he could release his grip and reach for his Colt, another shot cut the air and the Kid's body jerked as the slug plowed into him.

Longarm had his gun hand free now. He let the Stovespit Kid's body fall forward, down the steps, as he whipped his Colt out of its holster. His eyes were flicking along the street, looking for the source of the shots. As he brought up the Colt he saw a buggy across the street a short distance from the entry, heading slowly away from the jail.

A hand holding a revolver was sticking out of the buggy, but the vehicle's top was up. All that Longarm could see was the hand with the pistol in it and the brim of a derby hat above it. He triggered off a shot as the buggy started moving faster. The hand and the gun had now disappeared. Longarm let off another shot at the buggy. It was moving faster now, swaying from side to side on the deserted street.

Behind Longarm, the door of the jail burst open. Two of the jail deputies rushed into the entry. Both carried revolvers. They stood for a moment, trying to decide what was happening.

"One of you stay here!" Longarm snapped. "Tend to that prisoner. He just took two slugs in him. You—" He pointed to the second warden. "Come along with me!"

Longarm started running after the buggy. He saw the brim of the derby hat reappear, followed by the hand holding the gun. In the shadows of the high warehouse buildings that lined the street, Longarm strained his eyes trying to make out the distance-blurred features of the strip of face visible between the hatbrim and the hand holding the revolver. But the buggy was far ahead of him now, and he could not make out any details of the fleeing killer's face.

Muzzle-blast spurted, a streak of red from the bouncing, swaying buggy, but Longarm had started diving for the bricks the instant he'd seen the gun. As he landed and flattened himself on the brick pavement, the slug whistled through the air above his head.

The revolver's report echoed in Longarm's ears. As he brought up his Colt, the bullet from the buggy skidded along the bricks a few inches from him. A veteran of many shoot-outs, Longarm had registered the number of shots fired from the buggy. Even thought he'd been unaware that he was counting, he knew that there was at most one more round in his assailant's pistol, while he had three left.

Leaping to his feet, he started running after the buggy. Behind him he heard the thunking footfalls of the jail deputy. The buggy swayed as its occupant reined the horse into a cross-street, but Longarm did not slacken his pace. He reached the corner and saw the buggy, swaying as it gained still more speed, bouncing on the uneven paving between the huge towering sheds that lined the street.

Suddenly the cowcatcher of a locomotive appeared between the two closely spaced warehouses the buggy was passing. Longarm saw what must happen, but was powerless to prevent it. The buggy's front wheels rose from the ground as they hit the tracks, and while they were still in the air the locomotive's slanting cowcatcher smashed into the buggy.

Sliding up the slanting cowcatcher, the light vehicle rose from the ground. As the train kept moving inexorably forward, the body of the fragile buggy was crushed like an egg crate in a giant vise between the locomotive's boiler and a corner of one of the warehouses.

Longarm kept running. He reached the buggy before the engineer and fireman leaped from the engine cab, before the warden following him could get to the spot. He made a single running leap to the catwalk that extended along the locomotive's side. Now he could see that one arm of the buggy's occupant was protruding from the smashed buggy. The hand still grasped the pistol. Kneeling on the catwalk, Longarm peered through the narrow space between the end of the locomotive's boiler and the warehouse wall.

Ellie's eyes met his. They were protruding, staring blankly ahead. For a moment he thought she was dead. Then her eyelids closed, she shook her head, and she opened her eyes again.

Ignoring the trainmen who were coming along the catwalk, Longarm asked, "Ellie? How bad are you hurt?"

"I—I don't know, Longarm," she replied, her voice a hoarse, throaty whisper. "I don't feel anything at all."

A trickle of blood gushed down her hand. After the first burst had subsided, blood began dripping from the barrel of the revolver that she still held. Longarm glanced at the wreckage of the crushed buggy and saw the crash had folded it into a crease, as his hand might fold a sheet of cardboard. Ellie was jammed into a narrow vee made by the body and the seat. He looked at the blood flowing down her arm and knew instantly that Ellie had only a few minutes of life left to her unless she was freed at once from the wrecked buggy.

"You just hang on," he said. "I'll see what the trainmen and me can do to get you out."

Standing up, Longarm turned to the engineer and fireman. They were already shaking their heads hopelessly.

"We'd better get busy and get her outa there," he told them. "From the way she's bleeding, that big artery in her arm's been ruptured. She'll bleed to death if we don't get her free in the next minute or two. Can you back the engine away and—"

"This loco's not going to move an inch," the engineer said slowly. "I looked at the pilot wheels before I climbed up here. They're off the track and the rails are spread."

"But the drivers are still on the tracks!" Longarm protested. "And you still got up steam!"

Shaking his head, the trainman told Longarm, "Those drivers aren't anything but dead steel now. They're locked to the pilot wheels and piston. The only way this hog's going to move is for another loco to drag it free."

"Go back to the cab and try, anyway!" Longarm urged.

"All right, but it won't do any good," the engineer said as he motioned to the fireman and turned away.

Longarm dropped to one knee beside Ellie again. Before he could speak, she said, "I heard them, Longarm. I guess I'm not really afraid to die. Maybe it's better if I do."

In spite of the series of shocks he had received, Longarm was still thinking with his lawman's mind.

"You killed Jed, didn't you, Ellie?" he asked.

"Yes. He cooled down on me a long time ago. I knew when he stopped loving me, but I managed to get along with him, even if he didn't care about me any more. But when I found out he'd taken up with another woman I decided to shoot him."

"And the Stovespit Kid wasn't anywhere around the saloon, was he? You just waited until Jed came out and shot him."

"I was afraid you'd figure that out when you told me that Billy Vail had gotten word about the Stovespit Kid being in jail way out in Idaho when I shot Jed."

"You didn't have to try to kill me and the Kid, though," Longarm told her. "You were free of Jed, and likely nobody'd ever have tumbled to you being the one that killed him."

"I—I guess I went a little bit crazy," Ellie replied. Her voice was weaker now, a thready whisper. "That was me who shot at you the other night, too. But I guess you've already figured that out by now."

"It all came clear to me when I saw it was you in that buggy a minute ago."

"I'm sorry, Longarm," Ellie sighed. "Don't think too bad of me when . . ."

Her words trailed away into silence and her eyes rolled up. Longarm remained motionless for a moment, then closed her lids with a fingertip before getting to his feet and dropping off the catwalk.

"I'll say this for you, Long," Billy Vail remarked. They were sitting at a table in a back corner of the Windsor Hotel's barroom. "When you close a case, there's damned little left for me to sweep up."

"Meaning the Stovespit Kid, I take it?"

"Well, he's dead, so we don't have to worry about him getting away. And you won't be chasing after him again."

"I wouldn't be too sure, Billy," Longarm replied. "That man was so slick at getting away it wouldn't surprise me none if he pushed through them batwings right now, dragging his coffin behind him."

"You sound like you're sorry," Vail frowned.

"Oh, he give me a run for my money. And was I the kind to be a griever, it's Ellie and Jed I'd be thinking about, not the Kid. I guess it was like Ellie told me before she died, she went a little bit crazy."

Vail had just taken a sip of whiskey from his glass, and he swallowed before replying. "That's one way of looking at it," he said. "But I think there's another way to say what happened to Ellie."

"Oh? What's that?"

"It's something I heard some actor say on the stage a long time ago," the chief marshal told him.

"I guess you remember it, then?"

"I don't suppose I'll ever forget it, because I've seen it proved so many times," Vail replied.

"Mind telling me what it is, Billy?"

Vail shut his eyes and tilted his head back, then said slowly, "'Heaven has no rage, like love to hatred turned, nor Hell a fury, like a woman scorned.'"

Longarm nodded slowly. "I don't know much about plays and poetry and such, but I'll say this much. The fellow that wrote that was no damn fool. Now see if you can catch that waiter's eye to get us a refill, Billy. And this time it's on me."

LONGARM

Explore the exciting Old West with one of the men who made it wild!

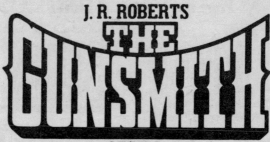

J. R. ROBERTS
THE GUNSMITH
SERIES